THE CURSED DIARY OF A BROOKLYN DOG WALKER

by Michael Reyes

Nightmare Press
Louisville, KY

There's something strange going on in Brooklyn. Occult chants ring out in the dead of night from quaint brownstones and trendy coffee shops. The stench of blood-soaked orgies and human sacrifice wafts through yoga studios and food co-ops. The servants of the demon star have come to power. And they are hunting for the only soul that can destroy them.

Thank you for reading! If you like the book, please leave a review on Amazon and Goodreads. Reviews help authors and publishers spread the word.

To keep up with more Nightmare Press news, join the Anubis Press Dynasty on Facebook.

For my old neighborhood and its ghosts

Other works by Michael Reyes

Praise for *Clock's Watch*

"I really liked the stories themselves. The various demons and monsters were interesting and creative. The stories were also wrapped up in a good manner with each one self-contained."
-Sci-fi & Scary

"Reyes' riotous creativity is almost overwhelming. So much weirdness goes on that, even though most of it's explained, it's difficult to really understand. Oftentimes, that sort of writing just irritates me, but here it's incredibly valuable at creating the sense of a deep and dangerous world that lurks below the boardwalk and inside dirty motel rooms along the Brooklyn shore."
-Black Gate Magazine

"One of the things I liked most about these stories is the prose itself. It has such a lovely rhythm to it and made for a great reading experience. Overall, I was pleasantly surprised by how much I enjoyed these stories. Honestly, this isn't really something I normally would have expected myself to like as much as I did. I would recommend Clock's Watch to lovers of dark fantasy, or folks that maybe want something a little different."
-Way Too Fantasy

The Black Veldt

"Get ready to be taken to some dark places when reading The Black Veldt. The story takes place during the Son of Sam murders, and author Michael Reyes does an excellent job portraying New York City in all its depravity during the mid-seventies. His writing style is sharp, witty, and not for the faint of heart."

"A very dark, well-written book."

"Black Veldt starts off dark and gritty – and never turns back! Don't get comfortable with where it starts, in a sci-fi/horror-painted canvas, because that's not where you'll be spending most of the time. (Don't worry, we get back there though.) Most of the POV is from 1970s urban New York, described to the hilt in all its underworld 'grandeur'; not to mention all the great music references of the time. Well-crafted and fully engaging!"

"I enjoyed this book it evoked a quality of writing like Clive Barker and felt dreamy like the Phantasm film got together in New York City during the Summer of Sam. It was a great ride and a strange delight to be inside the head of the narrator. Oh, and as a side note I will never hear an ABBA song the same way again."

THE CURSED DIARY
OF A BROOKLYN
DOG WALKER

by Michael Reyes

I
DRIED BLOOD
AND
BANANA BERRY SMOOTHIE

The Moleskine diary was covered in dried blood and Banana Berry Smoothie. It lay in the middle of an obscure trail in Prospect Park, and it waited patiently for him. The journal was small and Oxide Green, wedged tightly inside the dirt covered Jamba Juice cup. Its crusty bookmark ribbon poked out stiffly, lying along the ground like a dead possum's tail. Ants trying to excavate it died at the cups rim, and the rat attempting to bite the bookmark ribbon chewed its own arm off instead. No birds flew above it.

The Chow Chows weren't afraid. And they weren't affected. Iago sniffed it. King Kong bit it. Little Dirty Bastard lifted his leg to take a piss on it, then changed his mind at the last second. He back kicked it hard. It hit Jesse's scuffed up New Balance sneaker and took a hard bounce off to his left side, spinning in front of an Oak tree with the expression "Bob ♥ Men on Bare Back Hill" knifed into it. The Jamba Juice cup stopped spinning. The diary slipped out halfway. This is how it began for Jesse Ventura. The Chow Chow brothers quickly moved on. They decided to attack a fat squirrel laying low under the shade of an Elm tree. They barked loudly and bolted hard off the trail, their leashes almost ripped out of his grip. The dog walker went along for a short ride. His eyes never left the strange object, however, even as his black satchel swung around his neck. The strap choked the dog walker for a moment, and he quickly ripped it away from his throat.

"Heel!" The brothers stopped on a dime. Jesse continued to gaze at the small book. He slowly remembered that they were alone on top of the hill. The brothers were free to roam. The dog walker abruptly let go of their leashes.

"Go!" and the Chow Chows instantly bolted after the squirrel.

Jesse readjusted the satchel's strap on his left shoulder. He took a small joint and lighter out of his jacket and lit up. The dog walker took a few quick puffs then clipped the joint, carefully placing it back inside the interior pocket of his bright red flannel jacket. Jesse absentmindedly flicked the Zippo a few times, then he put that away as well. He couldn't stop staring at the diary.

Jesse walked toward it. He looked down at the crusty book, and felt an undeniable sense of déjà vu. A strong gust of chilly wind whipped orange and red leaves down around his shoulders. They fell in odd serpentine forms near the diary-filled cup. Jesse couldn't look away. An electric sensation coursed through him, his pulse quickened and his face flushed. There was the faintest twitch of an erection in his olive-colored cargo pants.

"What the fuck?" he muttered, disturbed by his body's reaction. His voice sounded far away, muffled, as if he was speaking under water. Jesse looked around suspiciously at nothing in particular. He struggled to regain his composure.

"Maybe it's a lost Bruce Chatwin journal. Recollections on Bare Back Hill in the Land of Park Slope." He stared up the trail. "Not a very good joke, huh, Little Dirty Bastard? I don't hear you laughing."

The Chow Chow instantly stopped chasing the squirrel at the sound of his name. He turned to look at Jesse, confused. Little Dirty Bastard halfway trotted toward the dog walker, tongue lolling out of the side of his mouth. "I was just making small talk, LDB. Do what you were doing. Go."

The Chow Chow obeyed, rejoining his two brothers in their hunt for the elusive rodent. Jesse looked back down at the half-revealed diary. A little more himself, but still fixated. He took a plastic poop scooping bag out of his black satchel, then bent down and pulled the diary out of the cup. It came out almost too easily, seeming to jump into his hand. He stood and looked at its filthy cover.

"Gross."

He stared at the spots of dried blood.

"This isn't just fucking Jamba Juice jam."

The dog walker suddenly felt as if he was being watched. He looked at the woods hugging the bike path intently. This obscure trail was sometimes used for gay cruising during the warmer months, but it was almost always empty during fall and winter. He listened carefully for whispers or moans but heard nothing. Still, Jesse felt like he was being spied on. Maybe a Park's Department Ranger had suspected something and stalked him from the Long Meadow. Jesse continued to listen closely, and continued to hear absolutely nothing. A chill then ran up his spine.

The dogs had stopped barking. The woods were unnaturally quiet. There seemed to be no sound whatsoever.

Jesse looked up the trail. The Chow Chow brothers were sitting together in the middle of the path. Iago held one half of the bloody squirrel in his mouth, King Kong the other. Little Dirty

Bastard looked like he wanted to bark, but he didn't. They were all gazing solemnly at Jesse. A strong wind blew silently in from the north. The dog walker looked up at the sky.

He saw nighttime constellations in broad daylight. It didn't look right— the bright clusters of familiar stars he couldn't name burning across the blue sky. The dog walker watched as two large clouds drifted toward one another. One resembled a serpent, and it came in hard from the east, like a cobra springing out of a snake charmer's basket. The other cloud moved much slower, serenely almost, canine shaped at first, then morphing into something resembling a latchkey. The two clouds collided and disappeared into a shapeless mass. They blocked out the strange stars. When the clouds parted the constellations were gone. Jesse Ventura looked away from the sky. The dogs were still staring at him.

"What the hell, man," mumbled Jesse, realizing he was higher than he had any right to be. The diary was vibrating in his hand like a cell phone. The unnatural silence continued in the public park. No birds chirped; no chill wind rustled autumnal leaves across the dry dirt.

Jesse Ventura opened the diary. It stopped moving. The numbers ′16° 43′ in print were stamped on the top page in black ink. 10/22, eight days ago, stamped underneath. Jesse squinted hard at the first page. No year, however, just tightly packed cursive that he could barely make out on the small white paper. Only a few sentences were legible:

I should hang myself with this dog leash. I curse the star above me and curs that walked me. Then two unintelligible sentences later: *If you're reading this you're now the one.* Then the bottom of the page: *They'll be searching for you; their spies are always on the ground.*

Jesse looked up from the diary. The three brothers barked then ran after one another playfully, leaving the dismembered pieces of the squirrel in the middle of the bike path. The natural sounds of the park were back, and they were so loud that he instantly doubted that they had gone away in the first place. Jesse looked at the diary again. He tried to turn the page, but couldn't. They were meshed together, and despite the diary's gross, sticky exterior the pages weren't stuck because of any liquid. They were held in place by some invisible force. He tried to turn to the last page, but it was inseparable from the back cover. All he had was that bizarre first page, and he couldn't make out most of the writing no matter how hard he tried. Still, the energy that coursed from it was undeniable. He feared it, and he didn't understand it, but the dog walker knew right then that he couldn't part with it.

Jesse took out some napkins and wiped it clean as best he could. For a moment it gleamed like bright metal, and then its texture seemed to change. It felt like warm flesh. Jesse shook his head. Did Marvin put PCP in his hydro? Jesse didn't feel like fighting a tree or rolling around on the dirt to get the spiders off, so he probably wasn't on angel dust. No, but something was up. The diary looked and felt normal once again.

Maybe he was in the middle of a weird interactive theater piece and he didn't even know it. This was Brooklyn, after all. *Jesus Christ, I'm probably being recorded*, thought Jesse. He looked around the trail again. The Chow Chow brothers were attempting to massacre another squirrel. He stared up at the sky and saw nothing strange. Jesse put the diary inside his flannel jacket. He heard a hiss from below.

Jesse looked down. The diamondback rattled its tail violently. He dropped the dirty napkins and a cold wind promptly blew them away. The dog walker scurried back and hurled his poop scoop bag. The serpent easily dodged the throw. Jesse glanced at the Chow Chows up the bike path. They barked and ran protectively toward him.

"Heel! Heel!" he shouted desperately as Little Dirty Bastard and King Kong barreled toward the viper. Iago darted into the woods next to the diamondback, ready to attack its flank.

"Heel!"

The three brothers reluctantly obeyed. Then growled and barked wildly. The viper paid them no mind. Its attention was completely fixed on the dog walker. The snake's head was raised high above its coils, and its long thick body was in the shape of an *S*. The diamond-shaped patches on its back seemed to glimmer under the milky autumn sun. The serpent's tail shook frantically, the rattle made Jesse's brain dizzy with fear. It scraped against the inside of his skull, looking for a way out. His brain didn't want to make sense of this.

They'll be searching for you; their spies are always on the ground.

The dog walker met the rattlesnake's gaze. It was hypnotic, and he felt paralyzed. A strange wave of energy from the diary compelled Jesse and gave him the courage to risk breaking away from the serpent's hypnotic stare. Jesse forced himself back. The snake hissed and jerked forward. King Kong made as if to lunge for it, and Jesse screamed "Heel!" once again. He then broke into action instantly. The dog walker turned left and sprinted down the trail, quickly hailing the three dogs. They ran to him. Jesse promptly hooked the brothers to his waist leash harness.

They turned and continued to growl at the large diamondback.

The rattlesnake bit down hard on the empty Jamba Juice cup and spit a stream of venom into the air. The diamondback raised its head, cup in mouth, fangs plunged deep into the container.

It turned to stare at Jesse once again.

"New to Brooklyn? Something tells me you ain't from around these parts. Get ready to say hello to Instagram, asshole."

The Chow Chow brothers secure, Jesse fumbled through his satchel. He looked away from the diamondback for a moment, quickly grabbing his phone. The dogs suddenly jerked forward, barking wildly. He dropped it.

The brothers stopped pulling Jesse back up the hill. They went quiet. The snake was gone, along with the cup.

Jesse shook his head in disbelief. He picked up the remains of his shattered phone and placed them in his bag. He looked down at the dogs. No longer fierce, they were now whimpering loudly. They continued to stare at the spot where the diamondback had been only seconds before.

"You guys ok?" he asked, reaching down to pat their heads. They barked and jumped up onto his waist. He eyed the bush next to them warily. "Let's get you guys home," he said, quickly running them down the bike path and off the hill.

Jesse touched the diary in his pocket, and it radiated a strange warmth. The dog walker looked back over his shoulder and saw nothing. Jesse Ventura didn't look up at the sky.

A thin, snake-shaped cloud drifted overhead, and it trailed the dog walker as he rushed out of Prospect Park.

II
THEIR MALEFICENCE IS INCREASED

Jesse sped into the foyer of the large two-bedroom apartment, pulse and mind still racing. He locked the front door and turned to see his client standing several feet away. Claudia was home from work early. The yoga instructor almost made Jesse instantly forget the psychotic weirdness he'd just experienced. Her deep blue eyes sparkled. She smiled at him. Jesse unhooked the brothers. They raced over to their owner, tails wagging frantically.

Jesse stared at Claudia Summers, and his stomach tied in knots. Her light blonde curls bounced on her bare shoulders. Claudia was still in her tight tank top and yoga pants. Every curve of her body gracefully tested the elasticity of her clothing. Jesse could smell the sweet mix of her perfume and sweat, and his head swam.

"How were they?" Claudia's voice was light and melodic. "Feisty. As usual," answered Jesse. Little Dirty Bastard began humping her leg.

"Bad boy!" she said, pushing the Chow Chow away.

11

"He's been really horny all day," said Jesse without thinking.

Claudia stared at him and said nothing. "I mean, not anymo— " Jesse cut himself short, realizing that the string of nonsense words about to fall out of his mouth weren't forming in his mind. The butterflies in his stomach were babbling, and they wouldn't stop going on about Claudia. He looked away from his client.

She had a movie playing in the living room. He could make out bits of dialogue. It sounded vaguely familiar. Claudia smiled at Little Dirty Bastard again and patted his head. He barked, wagging his tail insanely.

"He's a naughty boy! A naughty boy!"

Jesse stood there, watching his most beautiful client while trying to temper his attraction. He'd been working for Claudia for nine months and he still couldn't figure her out. She was one of his wealthiest clients, and that alone in most cases would pigeonhole her in this neighborhood, one of the most affluent in New York City. The apartment was hers; she didn't live with any roommates. That made them worlds apart, in the class sense. Jesse lived with a drug-dealing, Dungeons-and-Dragons-obsessed roommate in a rundown tenement in Sunset Park, and he worked because he had to. Jesse was a college dropout from a shitty town in upstate New York, and his abusive parents had bred him far below the poverty line during the brief amount of time they had custody. Child Services placed Jesse in foster care when he was ten, shortly after his dad nearly killed him and his mom.

"I treat you guys too good! You're all too spoiled," Claudia said as King Kong headbutted Little Dirty Bastard across his shoulder. The smaller Chow Chow barked, and nearly slammed against the wall.

"Stop that! Stop bullying your brother. You're family."

The dog walker looked at Claudia's Cartier pearl earrings and diamond saturated Rolex. He unconsciously scratched the burn marks his parents had left on his body.

Jesse smiled as he watched Claudia play with her Chow Chows. They were both from different worlds, but he still liked her. Claudia actually seemed cool, despite her money. Not condescending and fake, like so many of his other wealthy clients, and kind of weird, in a way that Jesse found very attractive.

The Chow Chow Brothers ended their greeting abruptly, and Iago walked inside the living room. King Kong and Little Dirty Bastard trotted behind him.

"Follow Iago, dog walker."

13

Weird, Jesse thought as he looked around the spacious room overlooking Prospect Park. A black leather Bilsby living room collection by DWR over the hardwood floor and a late 15th century suit of Gothic German armor in the corner by the window. A large flat screen on the wall in front of the leather sectional and chaise. There were dozens of framed, Photoshopped pictures of Claudia falling through the planet Saturn hanging all over the parlor, and other photographs of the Chow Chow brothers running along bright beams of chakra rainbow. The large Georgian style mahogany bureau and giant armchair were next to a thin hallway leading to the rest of the two bedroom apartment.

Jesse finally recognized the movie playing on the expensive flat screen. It was the beginning of *Texas Chain Saw Massacre*.

He pulled his eyes away from the 70's era teenagers in the van and looked at a large poster of Mr. Furley from *Three's Company* on the door to her living room closet. It made Jesse laugh. Either Claudia was trying way too hard to be quirky or she was just a few ghosts away from building her own Winchester Mansion. Either way, it made Jesse feel all kinds of mushy for her.

"Hey Don," Jesse said, nodding at the poster. There was a small chakra chart above Mr.Furley's head, and Claudia's yoga mat was laid out in front of the closet door.

"You want the poster? I'll give it to you if you want it," she said briskly, not looking at Jesse as she grabbed her purse off the chaise. King Kong sat on the large armchair and Iago chased Little Dirty Bastard into one of her bedrooms. Claudia took out four one-hundred-dollar bills. She handed them to Jesse.

"I don't have enough space in my apartment. That poster is too big," he said, smiling.

"With all the money you get paid? Oh please. So what, you live in a basement studio in Staten Island or some shit? No space? I bet you'd take it if it was a poster of Chrissy."

"I'm not into blondes."

She smirked at him.

"To the best dog walker in South Brooklyn. The Dog Whisperer. We love you."

"You're too kind," said Jesse as he placed the money in his pocket. He touched the diary. It still felt as if it was slightly vibrating, tickling his hand. The world went out of focus a bit. The viper, slithering back into his head, rattled its tail before Jesse in his mind's eye. Jesse realized in a very conscious way just how attracted he was to Claudia. She had almost made him completely forget about the rattlesnake and the diary.

"You want some water?"

15

"Sure," he said, shakily. Jesse took his hand out of his pocket. The dog walker's fingertips were hot.

"Take a seat." She walked out of the living room and into the kitchen. King Kong, the muscle of the group, stared at him arrogantly. Jesse dropped his satchel and sat down on the chaise. He looked at the knight. Claudia bought it at an auction five months ago in Fairfield, Connecticut. Six feet tall and fully articulated, the silver armor shined brightly, and it held a black scabbard. The hilt of a bastard sword rose out of it. Jesse's eyes focused on the knight's bright gauntlets, and he touched the diary again. The surface felt metallic for a moment. The dog walker took his hand out of the jacket and stared at the knight's helmet.

Claudia once told Jesse that as a child visiting museums she would fantasize about opening a knight's visor and finding the love of her life inside. Jesse smiled to himself. The dog walker wasn't the most romantic person in the world, but he was sure he'd fit in that suit of armor a whole lot better than Claudia's douchebag boyfriend.

Jesse sighed and looked away from the suit of armor, he watched the flat screen. The doomed teens were riding in the van, and one was reading from a book:

"The condition of retrogradation is contrary or inharmonious to the regular direction of actual movement in the zodiac and is, in that respect, evil. Hence, when malefic planets are in retrograde...And Saturn's malefic, okay?"

The girl paused for a moment. She touched the pastel shirt of the male driver next to her. Jesse instinctively touched the diary in his pocket once again.

"Their maleficence is increased," she continued.

Jesse looked away from the screen and blocked out the dialogue from the guy wearing the hideous shirt.

Jesse thought about the strange constellations he'd seen in the sky. The event was unnatural, and it hadn't been inspired by a few tokes of hydro. The dog walker was sure of that. The weed was good, he was still stoned, but it wasn't *that good.*

Some of the patterns in the sky had also seemed vaguely familiar. Had he seen some of those stars as a boy, tied to the chain link fence with his dog, Smokey?

Jesse shivered and blocked out the thought. He looked at Claudia's mahogany bureau.

Jesse spotted something he'd never noticed before: a small clay statue of a naked woman holding a serpent staff in her left hand. Her eyes were huge and vicious, they dominated her lean

17

face. Long hair fell on her bare shoulders. The cobra staff she held was tall and imposing.

The dog walker looked at King Kong. The Chow Chow was asleep, but when he felt Jesse's glance he stared up at him alertly. Jesse looked at the statue again. Claudia walked back into the living room with a tall glass of water. She handed it to Jesse, and followed his gaze. He drank.

"Like it? Blake picked it up at a flea market in Soho."

Jesse scowled. It would have to be a gift from that scumbag.

"It's um, ok, I guess," Jesse lied.

"He said it's from Libya. Some ancient goddess. Her name escapes me."

He nodded, not taking his eyes off the statue. Claudia continued to watch him.

"Are you ok?"

Jesse straightened up. He glanced at her, finished his cup of water, then placed it on the floor. King Kong gave him a disapproving stare.

"Yeah, I'm fine," he said, suddenly feeling very high and not fine at all.

Claudia walked over to the sectional and sat down. King Kong leaped off the armchair and ran to sit down next to her. She patted his head gently. Jesse decided to not mention any of the weirdness up on the hill. He would alert the Park's Department about the snake after he replaced his

iPhone   later   on   in   the   day.
"I tried calling you. It went straight to voicemail."

"I dropped my phone. It's broken."

"That sucks. Go get yourself an Obama phone. They're still around. I'm sure you qualify."

He grinned at Claudia, then suddenly felt a strange jolt from the diary in his pocket. He touched it softly through the fabric of his flannel. Claudia picked up the remote and fast forwarded the movie. Leatherface popped up on screen, chainsaw in hand. She let the movie play.

Claudia looked at King Kong's snout. She frowned and patted it.

"His nose is a little red. What's up with that?"

Shit, he thought. Had he not gotten all the squirrel gore off? Jesse bolted up, quickly grabbing a napkin from his satchel. He scrambled over to King Kong and looked at his snout. A very small red mark. He wiped it quickly. The Chow Chow stared at him, confused. Jesse put the napkin in his pocket.

"Frogurt. He licked up some Frogurt."

"Frogurt?" She stood up, arms folded across her chest. Jesse backed up.

"I let them off their leashes up on a trail. King Kong got out of my sight for a second and ran off into a bush. I caught him licking up on some strawberry Frogurt. I'm pretty sure it was gluten free, though. For what it's worth."

19

She shook her head and frowned at him. Claudia was serious. The chainsaw screamed loudly as Leatherface chased a girl around his house.

"It's not worth that much at all, Jesse. I know you're amazing with them...but still, please."

"It won't happen again, Ms. Summers. You have my word." He patted King Kong's head; the Chow Chow jumped up and licked his hand. Claudia couldn't help but smile. She gazed at Jesse. Their eyes locked. The butterflies in his stomach got hot again, if he didn't get control they'd be babbling in seconds. He looked away quickly.

"Won't happen again. I've been a little zoned out. I haven't been sleeping that well. Working hard on that book..."

The girl on the television screamed. Claudia picked up the remote. She muted it.

"I love this movie," she said giddily. "Don't you just love it when Leatherface spins around with the chainsaw at the end of the movie, all bat shit crazy? She fast forwarded it to the film's final few minutes. She looked at Jesse again. "The young adult fiction novel?"

"Yeah. *Lizzie Santos: Chronicles of a Latweena Dog Walker*. Latinx young adult fiction is going to be huge, and you know I'm half— "

She smiled widely at him, a twinkle in her dark blue eyes.

"Yeah, yeah, yeah— I know. You're half Italian and Puerto Rican. But can we pretend your Latino side is Colombian? It's a little more, you know..."

"What?" Jesse stared at her confused and a bit uncomfortable.

"I'm just kidding! I'm kidding. Look at you with your little ethnic pride. If I had a quarter of that I'd get my own float at the Pulaski Day parade. You do look a little like Carlos Lehder, though. He was Colombian and German."

"Who's that?"

"He was a narco trafficker with Pablo Escobar in the eighties and..."

"Get her King Kong!"

The Chow Chow bolted up on the couch, he was confused, but he still growled at Claudia. Iago and Little Dirty Bastard poked their heads out of the hallway, staring intently at their master.

"You can't do that! What the hell, guys!" Claudia said, laughing nervously.

"Heel!"

King Kong sat back down, looking at the two, still confused. His brothers stopped paying attention, and Little Dirty Bastard chased Iago back into the narrow hallway.

"They weren't really going to attack you. You always got something funny to say, right? That's for cracking your corny jokes, Claudia," Jesse said smiling.

Claudia was still laughing lightly.

Jesse shrugged nonchalantly and shook his head. Claudia's expensive earrings shined brightly, and so did her five-thousand-dollar Rolex.

"What? Lehder was kind of a good-looking guy. A maniac, but a good-looking guy. Why are you acting so sensitive, Jesse?"

Jesse felt kind of insulted but still sexually aroused. The butterflies grated against the wall of his stomach. He stared at her lips.

"How close are you to being done with the book?"

"Close," said Jesse, lying. He was nowhere close to being done; in fact he hadn't even looked at the book in weeks.

Her eyebrows arched, and she pointed her forefinger up in the air. "I might have something to help you with your concentration."

Claudia went into her purse, took out a pillbox, and quickly opened it. She handed Jesse three capsules.

"It's not Viagra. Don't bug out on me, bro. I'm not saying you fly half-mast. I doubt that very much."

Jesse smiled faintly and bit his tongue. The pills felt like they were going to dissolve in his sweaty palm.

"Adderall, Jesse. Prescription pills. Great for concentration. They might just give you the lift you need to get over your writing hump." Claudia winked at him. Jesse put the pills in his pocket.

"Thanks... but they're not like, really addictive, are they?"

"Not for normal people."

"Define normal."

"And I'm the cornball."

"Just saying. Pills like this always have side effects. I'm not trying to catch nosebleeds and crocodile penis."

"What? What are you talking about?" She laughed and shook her head.

Jesse shrugged. "I've seen those commercials, you pill pusher."

Claudia turned and looked at the knight.

"He's on to us, Lance. Anyway. Maybe they'll help. Seriously. Gator dick."

"Thank you, ma'am." Jesse walked back over to the chaise. He picked up his satchel.

"So, you're all squared away about the schedule change, right? You got the email?"

"Nope."

"Blake and I are going to Hudson Valley for the weekend. We're taking the boys with us."

He turned to face Claudia. *Fucking Blake. That entertainment lawyer prick. That turtleneck-wearing Muppet of a man*, thought Jesse. He didn't seem like Claudia's type at all, but then again how well did Jesse really know her? He still wasn't close to figuring this woman out.

"Ok. Well I hope you guys have fun," Jesse said, not hiding his disappointment as well as he would have liked.

"The boys haven't really warmed up to Blake. Maybe a weekend with them will change that. You're going to miss them, aren't you?"

She was smiling at Jesse, and they were standing so close that he could smell the intoxicating scent of lavender and sweat on her smooth neck.

"You bet," he said hollowly.

"Well, we'll just be—" Claudia stopped talking as her cell phone rang. She answered it. "Hey Blake. Yeah, I got back a little while ago. I'm just paying the dog walker."

Jesse stared at her coldly. *The dog walker*, he thought. *That's all I really am, isn't it? I'm just somebody to practice your little lines on, right? You could never really take me seriously.* He glanced over her shoulder at the statue of the woman holding the serpent staff. King Kong rolled his eyes and laid his head down on his front paws. Leatherface silently swung his chainsaw all by his lonesome in the middle of the road. Strangely, Jesse felt kind of sorry for him. If Leatherface had been raised by the right family, he might have been loveable and well adjusted, like Corky, from *Life Goes On*. Big guy too, could have been one hell of a power forward on the Special Olympics basketball team.

"Yeah. He's leaving right now."

Claudia stared at Jesse blankly and nodded toward the foyer. He walked out of her living room, heart heavy. Claudia accompanied Jesse to the front door, opened it for him quickly. Then she lowered her phone and smiled.

"Bye bye! See you next week!" she said loudly as he stepped into the hallway. Claudia put the phone back up to her ear, and closed the door before Jesse could say goodbye back.

The dog walker stood in the hallway for several moments, staring at the beige door. He could hear Leatherface's chainsaw, but could also hear Claudia arguing on the phone with Blake. Jesse couldn't make out exactly what it was about, but he had a strong feeling it might be about him.

Jesse allowed himself a slight smile as he stepped away from Claudia's apartment. He checked his watch; it was around three. He had an appointment real soon with another client and his Basset Hound, Ginger. John Smith was a super-rich customer who always gave very direct written instructions on where and how his dog should be walked. He was a real annoying prick.

The dog walker took out one of Claudia's pills. He shrugged and swallowed one. Maybe he would get lucky, maybe Adderall was her way of saying Ecstasy. It would certainly help his day along, after experiencing all that weirdness in Prospect Park. He felt the diary's unnatural warmth in his pocket and he took that out as well. Jesse walked toward the staircase.

He opened the Moleskine diary.

Most of the words remained illegible, but the other pages that were bound together seemed looser now. He pulled the first page down, and could make out the top of the next page. Printed in the same bold black ink as the other strange expression were the words: CAPUT ALGOL.

He mouthed the words out loud, struggling to pronounce them. The dog walker suddenly heard a noise off to his right side, a creaking sound. He looked and saw the apartment door next to Claudia's home slightly ajar. Jesse couldn't tell if he was being watched through the dark crack in the doorway, but it certainly felt like it. Creeped out and suddenly aware that he was loitering in his client's hallway, he closed the diary and placed it back inside his pocket. Jesse jogged down three staircases and left the apartment building.

III
VICTOR TELLS THE TRUTH

The chill autumn air welcomed Jesse as he stepped out onto the street. A voice he had absolutely no interest in hearing greeted him as well. A raspy, antagonizing voice that came out of a person he often felt like strangling. Jesse sucked his teeth and rolled his eyes.

Can this day get any fucking worse? he thought to himself.

"Messy Jesse! Jesse Pink Man! Ace Ventura the Pet Defective!" shouted Victor Santos in his heavy Nuyorican accent. Jesse glared at his dog walking rival.

Victor was Puerto Rican and almost sixty years old. He stood off to the stoop's right side, loose grip on a large Rottweiler's leash. Victor wore a baggy gray tracksuit and an old Orlando Magic Shaquille O'Neal jersey. Large nineties' era sunglasses wrapped around his small, wrinkled face. Black cornrows spilled out from underneath his purple du-rag.

"Is that you, Victor? I didn't recognize you for a second," said Jesse flatly.

Victor smirked. The Rottweiler happily attempted to greet Jesse.

"Heel Pepsi," Victor said to the Rottweiler. Pepsi looked at Jesse then back at Victor. He obliged reluctantly and sat down.

"Hola puto. Se acabo! Venni Vetti Vecci! Shiza!"

Jesse stared at him blankly. Victor laughed and clapped his hands together.

"Oh, that's right. You don't speak Spanish like that! You only half Boricua...you fake ass…"

"I don't. But I'm pretty sure most of that wasn't Spanish, man."

"Yeah? Maybe I was trying to fuck with you! See if you do know Spanish. But now I know you don't! You think you slick, or something? Please nigga…"

"Yeah. Could you not call me that? And could you please not say it around me? I have a lot of clients around here."

They were across the street from the park, on the sidewalk of Prospect Park Southwest. They were surrounded by expensive real estate. The Citadel, a large apartment building with a doorman was on the corner, and it dominated the block. It towered over the B71 bus stop and 15th street F train station beneath it. There were a group of high school kids cutting school and hanging out around the bus stop. They were talking excitedly about Halloween.

"Why? What for! I ain't racist!"

The front door of the apartment building next to the dog walkers suddenly popped open at the word "racist."

An elderly woman with an eerie resemblance to John Lennon burst forth, staring around alertly. She wore horn-rimmed glasses, a black beret and a Barack Obama t-shirt under her open peacoat. The rival dog walkers glanced at her, then silently glared at one another. She walked past, staring at them suspiciously. The woman stopped in front of the bus stop next to the high school kids. She gazed back at the dog walkers. The teenagers stared at her mischievously.

"Word's going around that you're falling off, Messy Jesse."

"Yeah. Sure. I think you're going senile old man."

"I ain't old motherfucka!"

Jesse suddenly bent down; he clapped his hands together and smiled at Pepsi the Rottweiler.

"Come here, Pepsi! Who gave you that stupid name? I'm going to call you Big Mac!" The dog stood and tried to run toward Jesse. He yanked Victor forward. "Stop fucking around, man! Heel Pepsi!"

"Heel Big Mac," Jesse said.

The Rottweiler stopped instantly. He whimpered and stared at Jesse, eager to be petted. Jesse stood up and flashed a wide smile at Victor.

"Falling off, huh? Whose dog is that? And what are you doing around here? All your clients are in South Slope and Sunset."

Victor smiled back at him.

"You don't know me as well as you think you do, man. Nah bro. Got a custi in this building, baby. I've been making moves."

Jesse checked his watch. The diary seemed to vibrate in his pocket. He wanted to look at it again, to be alone with it.

"Whatever, man. I don't have time for you. I have an appointment with another client."

"Ok, pana. You better make all the money you can now. Because word is you about to lose a client. That yoga chick's boyfriend wants to get you replaced, baby. He don't like you. Nobody does!"

Jesse frowned. He felt like siccing Victor's own dog on him. The old woman wearing the Obama t-shirt walked past them again, up the block this time. She stopped in front of the building she had come out of only moments before, and continued to grill them.

"Where did you hear that from?"

Victor laughed loudly. The old lady coughed, then spat on the ground. Several of the teenagers by the bus stop suddenly ran past the dog walkers. The Rottweiler jolted up, barking loudly. The teens took out eggs from their book bags, and the lady screamed as they tossed them at her, knocking the beret off her head. The woman held her Obama t-shirt forward, so they would see it, as if it was a protective shield. Egg yolk splashed all over the former president's face. She ran back inside her building, leaving the beret on the ground. The teens laughed and ran up the block.

The two dog walkers paid absolutely no attention to what had just happened. The Rottweiler sat down on the ground again, looking over his shoulder, up the block.

"Ah...hit the nail on the head, huh? You got feelings for the blanquita. Ahh...you hittin' it? You hittin' it? You know word gets around at the dog run. Maybe he thinks you a little too tight with his lady. Ha-ha. You know I'm telling the truth!"Jesse thought about it. He didn't say anything, though. Would she have him replaced?

"Yeah, bro. You're history."

"Get him Big Mac!" Jesse shouted. The Rottweiler instantly turned and tried to bite Victor. He jumped back.

"Chill man! Call him off! Yo, chill Pepsi!"

"Heel!"

Big Mac froze, then sat down in front of Victor once again.

"You ain't right, man," Victor said, trying to catch his breath. He took his sunglasses off, and stared at Jesse with bulbous, brown eyes. Jesse cringed and stepped back.

"Jesus Christ. Put those sunglasses back on. You look like a fucking constipated frog."

A fat pink-faced man in a beige trench coat and black fedora suddenly stepped out of Claudia's building. Victor saw him, and he instantly leaped onto the stoop, Big Mac's leash in hand. He rushed to hold the front door open for the stranger.

"Coño!" the man cried out as Victor smiled ingratiatingly at him, bug-eyed and still out of breath.

"There you go sir, have a great day," Victor said stiffly, attempting to sound as professional as he possibly could. The fat man stared at him, confused and terrified. He looked at Jesse and shook his head. Jesse shrugged.

"Idiota estupido," the fat man in the fedora said with a heavy lisp.

He sped around the dog and off the stoop. The fat man trundled down the block, looking back nervously as he escaped down the subway steps. Victor watched him go, then spat on the ground when he disappeared under the street.

"Fucking cracker. Didn't even say thank you," grumbled Victor.

"You have some serious race issues, dude. I think he was Spanish, anyway."

"Don't call me a fucking dude! What the hell's wrong with you, bro? You can't say shit like that! That shouldn't be your slang, nigga!"

"Dude, he was from Spain, you ignorant shithead. And stop saying that word around me!"

"That nigga wasn't Boricua, Mexican or Dominicano you half-white yuppie!"

"No. I mean he was *Spanish* Spanish."

"Like Cuban?"

"Like European!"

"You're a racist, Jesse. You just want to talk about Europe."

"Me? Racist? You're the bigot!"

"Don't be mad at me cause you a mutt. You hater."

"You're such a dumbass, Victor. You make me sick."

"Bro, you don't even know your own history! With your stupid fucking gringo man-purse."

"It's a satchel."

"You're a fucking satchel!"

The two eyed one another hatefully.

"You little punk! You ain't hood like me! If I didn't respect Saul so much I'd kick your ass and have you run out of Brooklyn! If it wasn't for him your ass would still be workin' at Petco. And you'd still be bagging my Kibbles and Bits!"

Jesse grimaced. It was a known fact that Saul Cohen, a dog walking legend in Brooklyn, had discovered Jesse at the local Petco. He had been a stock boy at the time, and Saul, a regular customer had noticed Jesse's gift with canines. Saul got Jesse into dog walking. He gave Jesse many of his clients over the years, and when Saul mysteriously disappeared Jesse got all of his wealthy customers. He was in a coveted position, and many other local dog walkers hated him.

"Don't do me any favors, asshole," said Jesse flatly.

"Paper or plastic, paper or plastic! You better start practicing, bitch! You gonna be out the game, bro. Watch and see!"

Victor disappeared into the building with his Rottweiler. Jesse stood there for a moment, thinking about what he'd said. Jesse shook his head. Victor could be telling the truth about Claudia, in fact, he more than likely was. He put it out of his mind, once again focusing on the electric surge from the diary nestled in his pocket.

Jesse walked toward Smith's mansion.

He didn't notice the two blonde-haired stroller moms seated on a bench across the street. They watched him closely, occasionally snapping pictures of him with their phones. The mothers pushed their bugaboo baby carriages back and forth forcefully; when he was gone they looked at one another. The Park Slope stroller moms simultaneously stared up at the sky, checking for cloud formations. Satisfied with what they saw, they stood in unison and walked off with their strollers in opposite directions.

IV
A SECRET MUSEUM
ON BROOKLYN'S GOLD COAST

Jesse sat along Brooklyn's Gold Coast, on a bench across the street from John Smith's mansion. He was stoned and tranquil. His back was to Prospect Park, and he was a good two miles away from Bare Back Hill. Prospect Park West was known as the Gold Coast in the 1880s, it was big money even back then. The twenty-block long avenue had late-19th-century Victorian mansions, elegant townhouses in Gothic and Romanesque styles. The true gateway to Park Slope was Grand Army Plaza, and The Soldier's and Sailor's memorial arch was America's own Arch de Triomphe. The Civil War Memorial faced south, staring down the defeated Confederacy. It overlooked the Brooklyn Public Library and Prospect Park. The gentry crouched under its wide shadow. The elite lived here.

Maybe even a few one-percenters. John Smith was probably one. Smith was a relatively new client, and he had been referred to Jesse by a corporate lawyer named Wilkes. Smith's last address had been in Dubai. He was a real estate guy, properties all over the world, a bunch of money in the U.A.E.

In spite of all that (or maybe because of it) his mansion was understated, yet strange. Red bricked and covered in ivory, it was Victorian, but it wasn't. The building seemed to appear out of nowhere several months ago. It was one story, and it stretched back for nearly half a block, centered right in the middle of the street and flanked by two small townhouses. The dog walker's first thought was that a Southern plantation had abruptly burrowed out of the ground and settled in Park Slope. There was a weird French Colonial vibe to the place. Jesse had truly never even noticed the property before, he felt like it appeared with Smith.

The dog walker held the open diary in his hand. His mind was sharp. Adderall sure wasn't Ecstasy but it did make him feel good. Jesse was reinvigorated. He had managed to unravel some more of the sloppy penmanship on the first page. The diary definitely belonged to a dog walker, an insane one at that. There were weird repeated chants in between the straight forward address of the narrator. The voice did have a familiar quality, and Jesse was reminded of Saul Cohen. Could he have written this?

Saul had disappeared over a year ago, and Jesse, like most people, assumed he was living on some island paradise in the Caribbean. Saul had made a ton of money walking dogs for the wealthy in Park Slope, and had talked about retiring for many years. Maybe he hadn't. Could Saul have something to do with this? The dog walker shrugged. Saul was eccentric. Jesse wouldn't put it past him.

Jesse yanked at the inside borders of the diary again. He still couldn't figure out how to unravel and loosen the other pages. Still, being able to decipher the script was a start. Jesse looked at his watch. It was time. The dog walker put the diary back into his jacket, and he stood up from the bench. He jogged across the street.

Jesse knocked on the heavy wooden door, five minutes early.

Claribel Pendergrass opened it immediately. The middle-aged Jamaican maid had her hair pulled back in tight braids, and she stared at him strangely. Her normal expression was always apathetic when dealing with Jesse, she always stared past him. But now Claribel was studying the dog walker attentively, her gray eyes shined like bright pearls in the deep sockets of her fish-like face. She was trying to find something in his eyes, and he didn't understand what she was looking for. The dog walker stepped back, uncomfortable. Claribel's gaze darted toward the strange diary in his jacket pocket, as if suddenly aware of the peculiar energy streaming out of it. He swallowed hard. She stared him down again.

"Hi Claribel. Is Ginger ready?"

Jesse had expected to find Claribel in the foyer with the five-year-old Basset Hound, preparing to hand the dog walker her leash along with a copy of Smith's annoying instructions. Only the maid stood there. Had the dog finally refused to be walked by Jesse? He had occasionally met some dogs he couldn't quite gel with over the years, but none quite like Ginger. The Basset Hound was hard to control, and sometimes it felt like she wasn't even a dog, but more like another kind of animal disguised as a canine. Jesse was certain she would warm up to him, though. It had only been three weeks since he started walking the Basset Hound.

"Yes, Mr. Ventura. Please come in. Mr. Smith has left something for you, in addition to your normal instructions." Her accent was slight, and her voice was husky. Claribel's eyes narrowed as she looked away from Jesse pensively.

"Really? Ok," he said in surprise. Jesse had never been invited inside of the mansion, never even really got a good look at its interior. All interactions with Claribel occurred through the doorway. Even Smith, who Jesse had spoken to only once, had addressed him in front of the building. He was a tall, lanky gray-haired man who went out of his way to avoid eye contact. Smith was super nondescript and unassuming, the guy was amazingly bland. You forgot him as soon as you met him, but you got the sense he'd never forget you. Smith was unsettling in a deep way.

Jesse stepped through the doorway. He closed the mahogany door lightly but it slammed shut heavily, as if somebody pressed the doorknob from the outside. Jesse jumped. Claribel didn't. She just continued to study his face suspiciously. The diary was getting hotter in his pocket; it felt like it was issuing some kind of warning.

"Follow me."

The foyer of the mansion was huge, nearly as big as his apartment. There was a shoulder-high marble bust of a hermaphroditic David on an ebony table, and the floors were covered in onyx tiles with mother of pearl inlays and small fingertip-sized diamonds. The walls were a glacial white, and the foyer was freezing, much colder than the crisp autumn air outside. There were photographs on the wall. Jesse doubted they would be on display in any museum of modern art.

They were pure smut.

Blown-up giant framed photographs of money shots and bukkake scenes, depictions of S & M sessions and bizarre group sex. Dozens of pictures hung on the walls of the foyer. The quality of the photos was poor, like the kind of pictures you would find in an old cheap triple-x magazine at a grungy sex shop. None of it was even remotely close to being tastefully done.

Jesse stared at them incredulously.

"I'll take it that Mr. Jones is a bachelor?" asked Jesse shakily.

"At this time, yes. He has a large family, however. He keeps pictures of some of his kin in the foyer," she said flatly.

"What? I didn't hear you right."

"One daughter and several of his nieces and nephews are in the photographs on the wall."

Jesse shook his head, looking at a picture of a male dwarf fisting a morbidly obese woman.

"His family? You're messing with me, right?"

Claribel laughed shrilly and said nothing. Jesse followed the sound of her footsteps forward without looking ahead. She has to be fucking with me, he thought.

Jesse followed her into the parlor, and he slammed down hard onto its diamond encrusted tiles. The dog walker's teeth chattered, and as he took in the living room his mouth dropped. Any remaining doubts about Smith being an absolute weirdo were laid to rest.

The parlor was cavernous. Five thousand square feet, and every inch of it appeared to be covered with those diamond encrusted tiles. There was a drop off of several inches. If Jesse hadn't been gawking at the cheap pornography on the foyer walls he would have been looking ahead, and he would have seen Claribel abruptly shrink several inches. The dog walker's head swam. The room felt subterranean.

The walls were painted pitch black. The parlor was essentially a museum room, and as Jesse looked around he realized it was a bizarre one at that.

The diary in his pocket grew even hotter; it felt like it was vibrating again.

There were giant brass statues of men and women interlocked with one another in the throes of ecstasy, human from the waist up but serpentine below. Large canvasses in a wide array of artistic styles lined the black walls, and they depicted these creatures. Some images were sublime, most were horrific. Large glass display cases contained strange costumes. Some looked like they were constructed out of old newspaper and random trash; others looked like suits of oddly shaped armor, chiseled out of gemstones: raw cinnabar and moldavite. Something that looked like a tattooed suit of skin was on display, as well.

What they all had in common was one specific feature, something Jesse couldn't quite articulate even as he observed it. He slowly realized that the geometric proportions in every single piece he saw were perverted in some way. There was no real symmetry in anything, no matter how seamless and beautiful (because some were) a statue or painting might initially appear. There was always a warped angle at the corner of an otherwise flawless sculpture, a distorted aspect somewhere along the surface of a painting. The theme was calculated degradation.

A huge painting of a constellation hung in the parlor's center, above the kindled fireplace. It looked like the unnerving constellation he had seen in the park, and one of the stars in the painting seemed to actually blink. Jesse wiped his eyes and looked away at a large stone table with crude metal chairs in front of the hearth. There was an old television set on the table. It didn't look like it had an extension cord.

"What the fuck..." he whispered, staring up at the blinking star once again.

"You look as if you've had the wind knocked out of you, Mr. Ventura," Claribel said, sounding amused.

"Why does that painting blink?" he asked, looking away from it.

"What painting?"

"The one above the fireplace," he said, pointing up at the large mirror.

There was no painting.

"That's just a mirror, Mr. Ventura."

Jesse stared at the mirror blankly.

"This is Mr. Smith's private collection. He is a collector of rare artifacts."

He gazed at Claribel. She was standing by the stone table, studying his face once again.

"The styles look…"

"There's only one style. One vision, Mr. Ventura."

She smiled. It was hideous. An absolute madness projected from her light gray eyes.

"Mr. Smith collects objects from lost mythologies, from forgotten races that existed as legends before our most ancient ancestors kindled their first fire."

"Some of them don't look old at all," said Jesse flatly.

"Some are not. The vision of these cultures transcend time. One piece of its vital history may have projected only for a moment in the mind of a lunatic several weeks ago. A madman who had the spirit to carve out the truth of his own deranged mythology, and in doing so found the thread to a greater vision, resurrecting it once again. You are looking at artifacts that most people don't even know exist. Mr. Jones has a very good eye for this special kind of art. Sometimes these objects are hiding in plain sight, all around us. Some may look new, but rest assured, the force behind them is ancient: Pre- Atlantean."

Claribel gazed at his pocket, and he felt uncomfortable. She looked away and stared up at the mirror.

"Um, ok. Yeah, but like where does he kick back? You know? This place kind of feels like a cave, but it isn't his man cave. I know he's not watching ESPN on that piece of shit television."

Claribel turned around and looked at Jesse. She abruptly laughed. He nearly jumped back. It was a cackle, and even more hideous than her smile. Claribel stopped, and she pointed over her shoulder at a thin hallway next to the fireplace.

"The rooms beyond are more conventional, all fifteen of them," she said. "But you can't see them. You've been instructed to wait out here."

Sure. Conventional, he thought. Torture chambers, dead bodies, as conventional as any fucking medieval dungeon disguised as a Park Slope plantation would be. One that, for all of Jesse's knowledge, had not even existed on this street several months ago. The dog walker shivered, despite the nearly nonstop pulse of warmth from the diary.

Jesse wanted to split. Immediately.

"Is Ginger in one of those conventional rooms, Ms. Pendergrass?"

The diary in his pocket felt white hot, Jesse had the impression that it might burst into flame and set him on fire. Jesse was feeling it now, drugs or

45

no drugs. The madness of the day was getting to him all at once, right now in this freaky museum parlor. The dog walker felt like his head was going to   burst.

"She's busy in the wine cellar."

Busy in the wine cellar? What the fuck does that even mean? he thought.

Jesse shook his head wildly, and then he lost it. The next string of words that poured out of his mouth hadn't been said since he was an abused child up in Newburgh. They were words that still repulsed Jesse to this very day. Words that had once gotten some slim ray of affection from his drunken father, because it was a line in the only movie his parents had ever taken him to. His scumbag of a father had once thought it was cute, and had actually hugged Jesse after he said it. "Alllll....righty...then! Alrighty then! Alrighty then! Alrighty then!" Jesse shouted like he had Tourette syndrome as he imitated Jim Carry in *Ace Ventura: Pet Detective.*

Claribel moved back a bit, startled.

Jesse was having a major freak out.

"Allllll-righty then, Ms. Claribel! Can we get Ginger! Alrighty then, alrighty then, alrighty then!!! Gotta get going! Gotta get going! Alrighty then!!" Jesse felt like crying, but held back his tears.

Claribel was staring at him, bewildered. The look of curiosity and suspicion had left her face. She was seriously uncomfortable.

"Busy in the wine cellar? Is she crushing grapes? Or drinking them? Alrighty then?"

"Please compose yourself, Mr. Ventura. You're behaving oddly."

Jesse looked away from her, breathing heavily. Claribel walked over to the giant stone table. She picked up a small paper and a plain brown bag from behind the television and handed them over to Jesse.

The brown bag was hefty, it felt like there was a dog bone and chew toy in it. He placed it in his satchel without glancing in the paper bag. Jesse caught his breath as Claribel continued to stare at him nervously. He read the paper:

Mr. Ventura, Ginger is to be walked to 1st Avenue along a specific set of streets within the next hour. I've included a route on the back of this letter. She must be allowed to gaze into Gowanus Bay for some time. You must then feed her the milk bone I placed...

Jesse stopped reading and shook his head. He turned the paper over, and there it was: a drawn map, heading south. But weird. Instead of a straight path to the bay it zigzagged east and west, up an avenue and two blocks south, up two avenues and several blocks north. The trek ended

47

on a street named Hyades, by the bay. He had never heard of the street before. Jesse was normally instructed to walk her a block away to the park and only for thirty minutes at a time. The guy was a controlling fucking weirdo, but this was too much.

"Is he serious?" Jesse asked quietly.

"Mr. Smith is always serious."

He shook his head and read on:

...inside the paper bag. Afterward, play a game of catch with her (the toy as always, is inside the bag) and you will almost be done. Having finished the game of catch, tie her to a post and leave her there. An acquaintance of mine will come to pick her up. You are not to make eye contact with him or interact in any way. He has quite a spirited nature, and is inclined to random acts of impulse. I know this is not a normal request. It's inconvenient, but I have my reasons, which I cannot divulge. If you choose to not perform it you will still be paid your wages, but unfortunately your employment with me will end permanently. If you do, however, say yes (which I hope you will!), you will be paid a bonus on the spot and an additional amount (the same amount!) upon completion. You will also never be asked to perform this admittedly peculiar dog walk again. Claribel has the envelope.

John Smith

Jesse Ventura shook his head. Too fucking weird. He looked up from the letter into Claribel's expressionless face.

"Do you have an envelope for me?"

She quickly took out a manila envelope from her pocket and handed it to Jesse without a word. He could feel a thick stack of bills inside.

"One moment please," Jesse said, turning his back on her.

He took the cash out. "Wow...Really?"

200 Benjamins. 20,000 dollars, cash. For one dog walk. And that was just half of it. Jesse couldn't believe it. He counted the money again. He looked over his shoulder.

Claribel was gone.

Jesse looked around the strange living room. He put the money back into the envelope. Jesse walked over to the giant stone table and placed it down next to the TV. Was this whole thing some weird kind of game? There were probably surveillance cameras all over the place. There were *definitely* surveillance cameras all over the place.

"Claribel! Hey Claribel?"

Silence. The television suddenly turned on. He jumped back.

"What the fuck is this now. A snuff film?" he mumbled miserably.

It wasn't. Gumby and Pokey appeared on the screen, and they traveled across the surface of a Claymation alien landscape. Gumby was arguing with some weird red-haired kid sitting on top of a train with a rocket. Jesse grimaced and looked away from the TV screen.

"This whole world is mine!" proclaimed the child arrogantly.

"Well if that's the way you feel we're sorry we wasted our time on your punk planet!" screamed Gumby.

Jesse gazed at the envelope again. That was a lot of money. He looked around the room. The wood in the fireplace crackled. The mirror above it remained a mirror. Jesse shook his head, not knowing what to do. He walked around the giant parlor, staring at the statues and paintings. The pieces of armor carved out of gemstones were shaped like the strange letters of some foreign alphabet. Jesse wondered what type of body could even fit inside of them.

The body suit made of old newspapers and random trash had the same shape, and as Jesse leaned in closer to the glass display he saw the headlines and dates on some of the yellow newspapers.

"John Kennedy Jr. Wins Second Term," and the *New York Sun* article said   November 2001. Another that read "John Elway Gets Yanks into

Pennant," and the year was 1987." Blackouts Continue Across the City, Meteor to Blame— 1977. These were events of which Jesse had no recollection. The aluminum beer cans and other junk making up the suit were of product brands that Jesse had never heard of, as well. He scratched his head.

"Next time you land on a planet make sure it has no craters," Pokey said to Gumby as they sat in the spaceship.

"Roger,"   Gumby   replied.

Jesse stepped away from the glass and walked over to another display case.

There was something that looked like a Hazmat suit made of skin, and it was covered in tattoos. They were images of the same strange letters after which everything else was designed. Only the gas mask was different. It looked like the bird-shaped mask plague doctors would wear in the Middle Ages. It was still made of what looked to be skin, however.

A dozen of the costumes in total, in large glass display cases. There was a huge tapestry that depicted Jesus praying to his own image on the southern wall, between paintings of those strange serpent creatures engaged in some bizarre funerary practice. They were burying a man foot up in a dark field. Jesse walked on and saw a long table with deformed figurines carved out of Red Jasper and cinnabar. They weren't human or animal but a combination of both, and they stared at him with an intelligence that belonged to neither. He stepped away.

The room was now quiet. He looked back at the television on the ancient stone table. Gumby and Pokey were frozen on the screen.

Jesse walked over to the northern corner of the room. There was a life-sized statue of a small child, around five. It was amazingly realistic, down to the tiniest features. The boy looked Middle Eastern, and he was wearing a tunic and ancient-looking sandals. There was an expression of absolute terror on his small face.

The diary was practically beating against Jesse's chest, and even though he wanted to take it out he didn't. Jesse's gut told him not to.

He stepped back and looked away from the horrifying statue. The television suddenly played again. Jesse stormed over to the stone table.

Gumby and Pokey were standing on another planet, this time with a kid wearing glasses and playing an arpeggio on his piano.

Jesse looked up at the mirror. Its reflection was normal. He stared down at the envelope. *Fuck it*, he thought. This was a reward for the day's psychological stress.

The clay child on the screen was becoming demonic, growing horns as he screamed at Gumby.

"Get off my world! I never want to see you again!   Beat   it!"
"I'm good! I'll take it! Claribel?"

Jesse picked the envelope back up and held it over his head. Silence. He lowered the envelope. The television shut off as Gumby and Pokey silently gazed at the demonic child.

"Claribel...Anybody?" he muttered. Jesse suddenly heard footfall coming from the thin hallway next to the fireplace. Animal footsteps, four legged, though they didn't exactly sound like those of a dog. More like an insect. A giant, skittering beetle. He stared at the hallway as Ginger emerged from it.

The Basset Hound's tongue was lolling out of her mouth, and she greeted Jesse with a bark. The red leash was already around her neck. Finally, something he understood. She was a strange dog, but how could she help it, being around all this weird shit?

"Hey Ginger," Jesse said, reaching down to pet the dog's head. She licked his hand and barked, tail wagging back and forth. Ginger had never been this friendly.

"Done getting drunk in the cellar? Ready to go for a weird, creepy walk? How do you stand these people?"

Ginger barked. Jesse held the envelope over his head once again, he waved it slowly.

"I'm all in, Claribel! Sorry about the freak out!"

He stuck the envelope in his coat pocket. The dog walker took Ginger's leash, and she led him out of the strange museum through the bright pornography-filled foyer. Pictures of his family, huh? And Jesse had thought his childhood was twisted. He opened the front door and stepped out of the mansion, not bothering to close the door behind   him.

V
JESSE VENTURA WALKS GINGER

It had gotten much colder. Jesse zipped up his jacket as he walked a block west of Smith's mansion. Still, it felt so much better outside. The dog walker could breathe easy again; being out of the mansion was like being released from the grip of a boa constrictor. The diary had cooled a bit, but its pleasant warmth still radiated throughout his body.

As Jesse watched the frost spill out of his mouth he thought about the day's epic oddness. The dog walker realized how he would deal with it. He stopped walking. Ginger tried to pull him forward.

"Heel."

She kept walking.

"Heel."

She stopped and looked back at him morosely.

He took out two Adderall pills and swallowed them, dealing with it. Hell, if forty thousand dollars was his reward for today's spooky bullshit then so be it. This was his last walk of the day, anyhow. He started forward again. Ginger wouldn't move. She continued to sit and stare at Jesse.

"Come on, Ginger." She remained seated. "Come on Ginger!" She got up grudgingly, then followed him.

He began his trek to Gowanus Bay. Jesse walked two blocks west, and then south. The brownstone-lined block was empty. Jesse still felt like he was being watched. There were a few Halloween decorations up around some homes, but most were barren. Ginger led the way, and stopped to sniff almost every piece of shrubbery she came across.

Jesse sighed and thought about the diary as Ginger urinated on a maple. He wanted to take it out, but his intuition urged him not to. Jesse looked up at a second-floor brownstone window. He saw a woman's angry face dart away from it. A curtain was quickly drawn. Jesse scowled. The clear-minded Adderall high was being replaced before it even really started. His mind was in a fog.

"Come on Ginger," he said, leading her away from the tree and up the block.

Jesse walked south, and two blocks east. Then south again.

He still felt eyes on him as he walked the next few streets. The brownstones and townhouses took on a strange sentience in his mind. Jesse saw demonic faces along their windows and doors. They leered at him, more disturbing than the carved pumpkins on their stoops.

Jesse felt relieved when they ambled onto Seventh Avenue. The coffee shops and restaurants lining it had more foot traffic. His comfort was short lived. As Jesse walked by a Connecticut Muffin he realized that he was getting his fair share of weird glances from the passing urban professionals.

This was common, but not in this quantity, and in such a small amount of time. They seemed to be glaring at Ginger and Jesse, gathering something from him walking her. This had never happened before.

Jesse walked Ginger two blocks east by an American Apparel store. She decided to take a dump next to it. Ginger relieved herself loudly in front of a storefront mannequin wearing a pink t-shirt, blue skinny jeans and purple boat shoes. It took Jesse a moment to realize it was an actual person, setting up a display of two female mannequins. The employee laid the naked mannequins down on the floor, and he twisted their plastic legs up in a scissors position. The Nebuchadnezzar-bearded hipster turned around to gape at Jesse and Ginger, then he lay down next to the figures. He began to fondle the two plastic women while staring placidly at the dog walker.

Jesse shook his head and looked away. He stared across the street at a small playground.

A trio of stroller moms were sitting on a large bench. They gazed at Jesse. They wore matching black peacoats, tight yoga pants and Jimmy Choo stilettos. All in their early thirties, and seated in weird positions along the large, green bench. An Asian pram pusher was sitting on top of the back rest, and she swatted a small horsewhip around her shoulders. A fish-faced ginger-mom was seated beneath her on the left side, smoking an American Spirit cigarette. The third member of the stroller posse, who looked a lot like Billie Holiday, was lying sideways, next to the Asian woman's right stiletto heel. Her head was in her hand and most of her body was off the seat. The stroller mom's long legs dangled onto the playground's rubber mat.

Three Maclaren buggies were scattered around the bench, and they were empty. There were no children on the playground. Only the three women. Jesse shivered. He looked down and saw that Ginger was done. The dog walker took out his poop scooping gear, and he cleaned the mess up quickly. Jesse looked at the bearded man in the window once again. He was still lying there, but his expression had changed. He was now in a trance, completely captivated by Ginger's wagging tail. His hands continued to grope plastic breasts and   thighs.

The dog walker strode over to a garbage can and tossed the bag of shit into it, watching the three women watch him. The dog walker then quickly led Ginger away from Seventh Avenue and down to the next block.

He walked the next few avenues in a daze, zigzagging west and east while following the directions on the map. Jesse kept his eyes down, but he could still feel people inspecting him. The diary in his pocket felt like a burning stone. The dog walker glanced up from the pavement. This area was desolate. He was completely alone with the Basset Hound.

Brownstones and condos had become small one-story houses and tenements, interspersed with large amounts of dirt lots. Jesse was in the home stretch now; it was a straight walk from here. He put the map away. The dog walker loosened his grip on the leash and slowed his pace. They were two blocks away from their destination.

Ginger ran after a squirrel, barking loudly. He let her go. She bolted up to a sickly-looking elm and growled up at the rodent. Jesse smiled. This was healthy. It was the most vigor Ginger had ever showed Jesse. He took out his joint and lit up, inhaling deeply. Jesse coughed hard on the hydro, but he was comfortably numb within minutes. It would probably add to his paranoia, but he could live with that. Tomorrow he'd be able to blame all the weird events of this day on drug use. It was a reassuring thought, and one that just might help him keep his sanity. He clipped the joint then walked over to Ginger and picked up her leash.

"Come on, girl."

Jesse could smell the saltwater before he walked onto the avenue. The immediate area was industrial and deserted, but he could see some activity further west. A few passing freight trucks, but no pedestrians. Every other street was gated, barring entry to the canal. Hyades Street was the only open lane. He walked onto the small block. There were shuttered auto repair shops on each side of the street, along with one large warehouse on the left side. The structures tapered off going forward.

Jesse could see the brackish waters of Gowanus Bay. Its waves were calm. The area in front of it was littered with junk: ripped tires and weird chunks of plaster. There was also something that looked like a graffiti covered port-o-potty by the water, as well.

"Ok Ginger, this is it. This filthy place is where your master wants me to take you. This is your playground I guess," he said, looking down at the small Basset Hound. She looked up at him and barked. Jesse led her forward. The stench of the

Gowanus was powerful. "Gross," he said, wiping his nose.

Jesse continued. The light blue port-o-potty looked old, and it was coated with strange graffiti. There were pieces of plaster that looked like limbs spread around the assorted tires and scrap metal. The dog walker instantly thought of the statue of the Middle Eastern child in Smith's collection. Jesse sprinted with Ginger past the strange plaster. He took the letter/map out of his pocket, scanned it over quickly.

"Ok, Ginger. So first you 'gaze' into the bay and then I give you a milk bone. So get to gazing…"

The Basset Hound was already leading him toward the bay. She seemed fixated on something, though all Jesse could see was open water and not much else. Not even random floating trash, which was weird. Ginger stopped and sat on her haunches, quietly gazing at the gentle waves. Jesse saw what she was staring at. The sun's rays reflecting off the water's surface. They danced in strange patterns along the briny canal. The thought that she wasn't a dog crossed his mind again. Ginger swayed back, and there was something slightly reptilian about the motion. Her tail waved strangely, like a diamondback's rattler. The dog walker grimaced.

"Ok, girl, I'm going to leave you there to do your thing for a while," he said nervously, dropping the leash.

"Don't jump in now, ok?"

Jesse took out white milk bone and purple toy. He juggled them slowly, turning to survey the area. It was completely empty, and every structure on the block looked as if it hadn't been used in years. Jesse doubted he was being tailed, but was sure the chip in Ginger was being tracked by her owner. Smith probably had a fucking camera implanted in her forehead.

Crazy rich fuck, thought Jesse. He stopped juggling the milk bone and chew toy, quickly putting them back inside his satchel. Jesse figured it would probably be best if he played catch with Ginger away from the water, a little bit up the street. There was way less rubble. He looked at the strange garbage on the ground.

The scattered stone arms and legs were everywhere. The largest piles were by the graffiti-covered   port-o-potty. Jesse walked in front of it while taking out a plastic glove. He slipped it on his right hand, bent down to pick up a forearm. It was heavy, and its details were impeccable. Jesse looked at the thin strands of hair, the pores they sprouted out of. The craftsmanship was identical to Smith's statue.

After a few moments Jesse realized it didn't feel like plaster or stone. He couldn't really describe the texture. The closest thing he could think of was water wrinkled skin. He hurled the forearm against the ground. It didn't crack. Jesse approached the port-o-potty. The smell coming from it was horrendous, but it wasn't shit or piss. More like burnt hair and decay. A rotting body.

Jesse wrinkled his nose. He looked at the port-o-potty's graffiti. It wasn't typical. There were no tags, and some of the images looked like magical symbols. He thought of those weird costumes fashioned like strange letters in Smith's secret museum.

Jesse walked the portable toilet's perimeter. The words Caput Algol were written all over it in black marker, from top to bottom. The handwriting was small and tight, and it didn't deviate. One person wrote those same two words over a thousand times.

The dog walker took out the diary and turned to its second page. The handwriting didn't match the toilet scribbler's. Jesse quickly put the diary away, fingertips hot from its warmth.

"Jesus Christ. What's going on?" Jesse said, running his fingers through his hair.

Ginger suddenly began to howl. It sounded like a human imitating a dog. Jesse looked at the Basset Hound, and he stared in horror at her

63

shadow. It was leech-shaped, tentacled, and slowly pulling away from her stationary body.

The dog walker suddenly felt eyes on his back. He turned away from Ginger. Jesse saw over a dozen people scrambling noiselessly away from the block's corner. Ginger stopped howling. Jesse faced her again. The dog's shadow was now normal, motionless, and by her side. Ginger jogged away from the water. Jesse stumbled back toward the portable toilet. His head was spinning. *Why is all this shit happening to me?* For a moment Jesse felt like tossing the diary into the bay. But he knew he couldn't. Jesse touched the money in his pocket, and it grounded him. Forty thousand total. And soon. The diary suddenly burned hot against his chest. His mind raced, then splintered.

This is all an experiment. No – a ritual. They're watching me, and trying to figure me out. It has to be the diary. But how could they know? Who were THEY in the first place? The diary cooled. He pushed those thoughts out of his mind. They were all bullshit. He had smoked too much. It was simple paranoia.

"Let me do this and get the hell out of here. I got a treat for you, Ginger." Jesse practically ripped the milk bone out of his bag. He waved it in front of the Basset Hound. She trotted over to him. The dog walker was hit with a heavy sense of dread as he clutched her treat. Jesse felt an odd synergy with the animal, more than he ever had before. It frightened him. Ginger was possessed. There was a serpentine force coiled around the Basset Hound's spirit. Jesse looked up at the sky and felt those bright constellations shining down on him, though he couldn't see them. The clouds that passed overhead were formless and vague. He sucked his teeth, suddenly mad at himself. There were never any fucking snake and dog clouds. No weird stars. It was all drug induced paranoia. Or not enough sleep. The diary beat against Jesse's chest. He fought against its reality. Jesse placed the milk bone on the ground. Ginger sniffed it suspiciously. She looked up at her walker.

"Go ahead, girl."

She began to eat. The dog walker looked up the street and saw an empty avenue. There was no shadowy mob watching him. Jesse also didn't see any trace of Smith's "spirited acquaintance." So, what, then? Just tie Ginger up and leave her? Or was he supposed to wait for the person to show up? Jesse looked at the buildings. Maybe the person was hiding inside one, waiting for him to leave.

Ginger barked. It sounded strange, kind of like a hiss. He turned to face her. She looked nauseous.

Jesse got down on his knees to pet the Basset Hound.

"You ok, girl?" She wagged her tail and licked his hand.

"There you go. Now let's have a catch." He stood and took her squeak toy out of his satchel. Jesse tossed it up the street. Ginger gave chase. She brought it back and he flung it even further up the block. She ran after it again. Jesse turned his back and walked past the portable toilet, closer to the water. Ginger didn't follow.

The Basset Hound froze in front of the port-o-potty. She dropped her toy, then gazed at its door. Ginger suddenly let out a deep howl. She began to race around the latrine. He'd never seen Ginger run this fast before, never seen her possess so much raw energy. She was running furiously in tight circles around the port-o-potty, tongue lolling out of her mouth.

"What the fuck was in that milk bone? Meth?"

The Basset Hound was making strange noises that once again weren't quite barks. The sounds were guttural, reptilian. The dog walker approached her. She abruptly slowed to a trot, then stood in front of her toy, panting heavily. Jesse petted her head. He picked up the toy and put it back in his bag. The dog walker looked up the street. He saw no one.

"He wants me to leave you here alone? Like this?

She blinked heavily at him. The Basset Hound was sick and depleted. Whatever strange thing Ginger had in her was gone. Jesse was looking at a normal dog now. He knew it instinctively.

"Fuck the rest of the money. This is too weird. I'm not leaving you here." He grabbed her leash and began to quickly walk off Hyades Street.

The port-o-potty started to shake.

The dog walker snapped around. The portable toilet was quaking violently, as if someone were thrashing around in it. Jesse started power walking up the small block. The diary beat hard against his chest.

Ginger was starting to totter. Jesse was halfway up the block when the port-o-potty door swung open. It was Smith's spirited acquaintance.

VI
TREVOR JOHN

The man spilled out of the port-o-potty like hot guts from an eviscerated swine. Grotesquely tall and skinny, his legs buckled and his arms flailed. His rubbery neck swayed back and forth as his broad face glared up at the sky.

He wore a black Armani suit and Gucci loafers. His hair was blonde, and he wore it in a large pompadour. He was taller than the port-o-potty, by at least five inches. It was hard to see how he fit himself inside. He looked well over seven feet tall.

The strange man regained his balance. He still looked at the sky, and Jesse stared at it along with him. Long, white serpentine clouds raced overhead. Jesse heard Ginger's labored breathing. She was staring up at him sickly, her eyes bloodshot. Gobs of drool fell from her mouth. Jesse heard a sudden whistle by the latrine. He looked up. The man was staring at him. His face was odd, so large that it seemed to stretch his big ears to the back of his head. His wide mouth and broken nose dominated the broad expanse of his waxy white face. His large eyes were shark black, and his eyebrows were so blonde they were nearly transparent. The two halves of his face seemed incompatible. There was no real symmetry in the features; the left side of his face seemed higher than the right.

The freak smiled at him.

Jesse grimaced. The smile was repulsive. It nearly took up his whole face. His teeth were blindingly white, the bleached knuckle bones of a skeleton left under the desert sun.

Jesse couldn't look away. The razor-thin man kept that smile going for longer than he had to, for longer than any sane person ever would.

He suddenly dropped it. He waved to Jesse wildly, right hand fluttering like a one-winged bird trying to take flight.

"Hello, Jesse! I'm here on behalf of Senor Smith! I'm here to pick up that bitch! My name is Trevor John!" His voice was deep, and he had no accent. He pronounced every word carefully.

Ginger growled. Jesse looked down. The dog's legs were buckling. He looked up at the freak again. Jesse didn't know what to do at first. Then it dawned on him as he stared at the bizarre figure of the man-thing named Trevor John— that the freak was human shit made flesh. A fucking abomination.

Jesse gave him the finger.

69

"Go fuck yourself!" screamed the dog walker. His voice cracked a bit, but he didn't look away from Trevor John.

The grotesque man's reaction was instant. He jolted back as if hit in the stomach, then he did a strange slow hip shake, with his two thumbs pointed up at the sky. Jesse stared at him, bewildered.

"Fine! Have it your way!"

Trevor John stopped, then smiled again. He did something that shocked and repulsed Jesse so much that he nearly threw up.

Trevor John flashed him.

He whipped his cock out of his Armani pants, and it was grotesquely large and deformed. It looked like a pink python, beaten with a baseball bat. It was covered in welts, and it dripped.

Jesse held back bile. He looked away.

"Hey Pretty Boy! Don't be afraid of old Trevor John's ankle spanker! You think you're gagging now! Just wait till I get a hold of you! Wait until *we* get a hold of you! I know you're the one! They may not believe it yet but I know you are! You're headed to the snake pit! You're fucking dead meat! You can't stop her! Caput Algol! She will walk again! Caput Algol!"

Trevor John laughed insanely. He danced a little jig and swung his giant cock around.

Jesse stifled a scream as he ran up the street, dragging Ginger along. She barely kept up as he rushed past the empty buildings and onto the avenue. The diary was blazing hot, but it didn't burst into flame as he turned the corner. Silence. Trevor John's horrible cackling had stopped. Jesse was dragging the poor Basset Hound. He turned and saw that she was barely conscious. He let go of her leash as they stumbled onto the empty street, which wasn't empty for long.

"No!"

He saw the red Prius before he heard it, saw it suddenly bearing down on them from their left side. Jesse bolted and tripped onto the sidewalk. The car struck the Basset Hound. A heavy thud, but no yelp, and the sound of the driver hitting the gas and speeding away. Ginger was hurled toward Jesse's side of the street. She landed a few feet away from him.

Jesse screamed. He tried to rise, but his legs were in agony. He shut his eyes for a moment, summoning the strength to stand. The diary burned hot, and Jesse saw a vision of his old dog, Smokey. The Husky's blue and brown eyes sparkled. The dog walker felt a surge of energy.

There were suddenly voices all around him, the unmistakable murmur of a crowd. Jesse opened his eyes. The block had been deserted only moments before. Now there were throngs of people on the avenue, coming out of the decrepit warehouses and abandoned buildings, walking heavily down streets that were silent less than a minute ago. There were already two joggers standing above the battered dog, running in place as the other pedestrians converged onto the street.

Moms with strollers appeared, and he recognized one as the red-haired woman who had been watching him from the playground bench. She was surrounded by bi-racial artisans dressed in skinny jeans and Carhartt jackets. Hip, young lesbian couples with mohawks stood next to elderly white men in smart gray business suits.

Jesse counted at least fifteen people. He sucked up the pain and stood. Ginger was whimpering, alive, but barely. He stumbled over to her, legs in hot pain. Jesse shoved the two joggers out of his way. Ginger was covered in blood. The dog's stomach had been split open. Hot intestines streamed out of her belly. Jesse held back tears as he got level with her. She looked at him, eyes blinking slowly.

Jesse heard whispers in the crowd.

Is he the one? Take him now. No, not sure, we still need time...tests! Be safe, Take him now. Kill the peasant! No. He may not be. There isn't enough time....

Jesse didn't bother to turn around. Tears rolled down his cheeks as he watched the light fade from

the   Basset   Hound's   eyes.
"I'm afraid there's nothing that can be done for her,
Mr.   Ventura."
Jesse   froze.   He   recognized   the   deep,
expressionless voice at once.

"Smith?"

Jesse stood and faced his client. Smith wore a
black and white track suit and bright orange
running shoes. He stared at Jesse coldly. The
jogger next to him was a strikingly beautiful
Middle Eastern woman with deep set, sparkling
green eyes. Her long black hair was parted in the
middle. She was dressed just like Smith, down to
the sneakers. Her eyes bore into Jesse. "I'll take it
from here. You didn't keep your end of the deal.
You were supposed to tie her up and leave. I won't
be able to pay you the rest of the money. You're
fired, as well," said Smith.Jesse stared at him
blankly. He looked down at the dead dog, then
back up at her owner.

"I don't know what the fuck is going on here-"

"Perhaps   you   will   in   time..."   said   a
bespectacled stroller mom. Black bangs clawed at
her large forehead.

"What are you talking about!" snapped Jesse.

She went silent, pushing her empty baby
carriage back and forth. The woman received
disapproving glares from the crowd, and the
ginger-haired stroller mom from the park spat on

73

her shoulder, then smacked the back of her head. Her bangs shook and her glasses almost fell off, but she didn't so much as blink. Jesse began to creep away from the small mob, who were now all gathered next to Ginger and Smith. Jesse looked around for Trevor John. He didn't see him. "That guy in the port-o-potty showed me his cock! You set this up, Smith!"

Smith completely ignored the dog walker. Everyone did. Smith squatted down next to Ginger. He scooped up a hand full of her intestines, then he hurled them onto the ground. Jesse watched in quiet terror. The crowd stared at the splayed intestines along with Smith. Then they followed his gaze up to the sky. They looked down at the guts again, then back up at the clouds.

Jesse crept away, further up the street. The jogger with the bright green eyes stared at him once again. Her face was downcast.

Smith frowned and stood. He shook his head.

"Still not sure..." he said sadly.

The crowd began to repeat his statement and add their own comments. No one stared at Jesse. *Still not sure...Not the one? The disgusting peasant...He must be...He's not! The fucking loser...There is another way...We'll find out soon enough! During the right hour...Take him to be safe! Kill him; he knows too much! Let him go, nobody will ever believe him...He's poor...Gross...Nobody will believe him...ask him if he has it!"*

The crowd went silent. They began to nod their heads approvingly at a small, freckled bald man wearing horn-rimmed glasses and a Phish t-shirt.

Ask him if he has it! Yes! Ask!

The mob stared at Smith. He nodded at the freckled bald man approvingly.

"Huh. Yes. Ask him," said Smith, more to himself than anyone else.

The crowd began to slowly applaud the Phish fan. Jesse watched this horror show in silence. It felt like he was having an out-of-body experience.

The crowd was vigorously applauding the man. Someone blew an air horn. The Phish fan beat his chest. Smith told them to "quiet down," and they did. All at once. He then turned to face Jesse. Everyone else followed suit.

"Mr. Ventura...I'm afraid I might have been a little "passive aggressive." Not nearly direct enough for someone of your breeding and caste. I profile you as a "talk straight, meat and potatoes kind of fella." They say the easiest way from point A to point B is a straight line. This is a universal notion."

"Occam's Razor," said the Phish fan.

"Shut the fuck up! You're banned from all group activities for the next 48 hours!" yelled Smith.

"But tomorrow night!"

"Leave!"

The man began to tear up. Somebody in the crowd dumped a cup of Starbucks coffee on his head. He cried out, but quickly went silent. A stroller mom kicked him in the ass and he ran up the block.

Smith stared at Jesse again. "Did you happen to find anything peculiar today, Mr. Ventura?"

"You're fucking crazy."

Smith shook his head and smiled.

"Mr. Ventura. You didn't answer my question."

"Answer his question! You fucking gross poor person! You peasant!" a man shouted. He looked like the social theorist, Malcolm Gladwell. Jesse couldn't be sure; it might have actually been Malcolm Gladwell.

"Did you, or did you not...come across a strange object today?"

Jesse spat in Smith's face. The loogie splattered against the bridge of his nose with a satisfying thud. The crowd went berserk.

"Kill him! Kill the Undesirable!"

Jesse ran as fast as he could. The Middle Eastern woman next to Smith shook her head. She put her hand up.

"Don't chase him!" Smith yelled, while staring at the woman. He wiped Jesse's spit off his face.

The dog walker's pursuers stopped in mid-motion. The crowd went quiet.

"We'll find out soon enough," said the green-eyed woman in a soft Persian accent.

VII
THE DEMON STAR

Jesse was in a severe daze as he staggered from avenue to avenue. His adrenalin kick was over, and he was beginning to feel the pain in his legs again. He was now around more traffic and pedestrians, and he was thankful for that. Jesse had run blindly away from Smith and his mob, and he wasn't sure if he had covered a dozen blocks or three. He stood on a street corner, delirious and exhausted. Gypsy cabs cruised past him.

I need to get out of this neighborhood as quickly as possible.

The dog walker hailed, arm weak and bobbing. A black Lincoln Continental pulled up. Jesse swung open the back door and jumped inside. He tried to close it twice before realizing his bag was stuck.

"Your bag, sir! Your bag!" yelled the Indian cab driver.

Jesse nodded, then kicked the door open. He pulled the strap with two hands, and the bag shot inside and nearly hit the back of the cabbie's head. Jesse slammed the door. He looked at his right hand. There was still a plastic glove on it.

"Shit, man!" Jesse shouted in irritation. He tore off the glove and threw it out the window.

The cab driver stared at Jesse blankly.

"40th Street between Fifth and Sixth Avenue."

The taxi driver stared on and said nothing. Jesse took out a hundred-dollar bill.

"Do you have change for a hundred?"

The driver's face began to twist in anger. He snarled. "No!!! I do not have cha…"

"The hundred is yours. Please drive quickly." Jesse handed him the bill. He frowned, then snatched it. Jesse slumped back into the seat.

The cabbie stepped on the gas.

They drove in silence. Jesse gazed out the window, but he saw nothing. There was no regulating his thought process; the day's nightmarish images ran in a constant loop across his mind's eye. He almost cried out. The driver snatched nervous glances at his passenger. Jesse touched the diary in his pocket. It felt like a warm hand embracing his own. The electric warmth flowed. He started to feel a little better.

"This whole thing is a nightmare, and when I go to sleep I'll wake up back in my real life."

"Excuse me? Did you say something?"

Jesse ignored him. The cab passed into Sunset Park.

Jesse was beyond exhausted. He closed his eyes. The dog walker kept his hand on the diary, and he quickly fell into darkness. He suddenly heard Claudia's voice calling for him in that black chasm. She was in danger. And it was his fault. The taxi screeched to a halt.

"We are here."

Jesse opened his eyes and wiped the drool from his mouth.

He looked out the window. The front door of his six-floor apartment building was only a few feet away. The cabbie stared the dog walker down. Jesse yawned and stretched. Children getting an early start on their trick-or-treating walked with their parents along the streets, plastic pumpkins in hand. Jesse staggered out of the cab without a word. He slammed the door shut. The cab driver sucked his teeth.

"Were you expecting a tip? You just got $100 for a $20 ride, dickhead."

The cabbie glared at Jesse then sped off, leaving the dog walker in a cloud of exhaust. Jesse coughed and looked around the street, with its long line of drab apartment buildings and small two-story houses. There was no visible sign that he'd been followed. Jesse took keys out of his flannel jacket, and he opened the heavy front door. The dog walker stepped inside quickly, then pushed himself up three flights. He saw no neighbors. Jesse hoped he would have the same luck with his roommate.

He did.

There was no trace of Marvin Trout. Jesse walked past the turquoise painted kitchen and small bathroom toward the living room. In it sat a large flat screen, a heavy wooden table, and a worn black sofa. There were folding chairs around the table and Dungeons & Dragons gaming supplies on it—Marvin's stuff. Their bedrooms were next to one another. Marvin's door was closed. He was probably at The Den, a four-bedroom apartment on Fifty-Sixth Street.

Marvin and Jesse, along with three other people, contributed rent to that apartment. It was their crash pad, a place to throw parties and chill. Jesse staggered forward and jammed his key into its bedroom lock. The door swung open. Jesse stepped through, and back kicked the door closed. The room was spartan, a cot, writing desk and chair, a bookshelf next to a closet and a small window overlooking a dismal, asphalt backyard.

The only framed photograph was a picture of him with Smokey. Jesse was seven years old in the picture, and he was hugging the Husky. There was only the faintest trace of a bruise under his left eye.

The dog walker dropped his satchel and took off his jacket. He flung it across the room and it slammed hard against a wall. The diary fell out. He glared at it, then fell flat on his mattress. Jesse was asleep within seconds. The nightmare snatched him up like a demonic bird of prey.

The blinking star in Smith's painting was watching Jesse, and he was paralyzed by its gaze. The large canvas floated several feet away from the dog walker. He was in a dark, featureless space. Jesse tried to move but he couldn't. The star stopped blinking. A woman's face suddenly leered out at him from the painting. She had large, bright green eyes and dark Middle Eastern features. He watched the tips of her thick black hair harden and turn to green scales. They began to move wildly, serpents trying to yank themselves out of her skull. This caused her no pain. In fact, she seemed pleased. The woman smiled grimly. Her eyes commanded worship.

Jesse heard the howl from behind, and it freed him from her spell. Jesse turned to face Smokey. The dark gray Husky's blue and brown eyes shined like twin beacons. Smokey barked, and they were no longer in inky darkness. They were on Prospect Park's Long Meadow. The sun was riding high over the long stretch of emerald grass.

The Husky ran, Jesse followed. They ran for miles and never tired. They saw nothing but rolling green fields and blue sky. It was exhilarating. Jesse felt that it couldn't last; his heart was going to overflow. Smokey stopped running. They reached the edge of the meadow.

Saul Cohen was standing there, with his back to a thicket of dark woods. He stared at Jesse solemnly through his large eyeglasses. Saul was dressed in what was once a gray suit, and he was covered in blood from head to toe. His salt and pepper hair was still neatly slicked back, not a strand of it was out of place. The sixty-year old's boyish looks and sardonic grin were still present.

"I'm sorry Jesse, but you need to stop them. You're the real herald. I was weak," Saul said in his thick New York accent. Jesse tried to speak, but he couldn't.

"Very soon...When they complete their ritual they'll know you're the guy for sure. They already suspect. Your friend will guide you to their snake pit. Kill their leader, Jesse, before tomorrow. In the name of the great guardian star. It watches over you now."

Saul pointed up at the sky. Jesse looked to the heavens, and saw a steadfast constellation. Bright. Fixed. Sirius. Jesse looked down at Saul again. There was now a blizzard in the woods behind the dead dog walker.

"They want to incarnate an essence of the Demon Star; Caput Algol, into a mortal woman. They want to resurrect a shade of the Gorgon. They're very wicked people, Jess. Murderers, sexual degenerates. Very, very bad people. They practice human sacrifice, bizarre sex magic.

They're Algol Egregor. They've worshiped the lowest principle of the Serpent for eons. They've elevated its darkest aspects, and only its darkest aspects. They're big time scumbags, Jess. They believe destroying this world and incarnating the Demon Star will make them immortal. Only you can stop them, and their hour is near. The conjunction is tomorrow, Jesse. The diary you carry is a living thing, it's not inanimate. It's a badge, it's a weapon. I was a coward, I failed."

Saul shook his head, and it fell off his shoulders. He caught it with his left hand and held it forward. Jesse would have screamed if he could have. Saul spoke.

"You can't let *this* happen to you, Jess. That fucker Trevor John did this to me. He's not completely human. Succeed where I failed! Embrace Ishum, the messenger of Sirius. It'll reveal everything to you when you accept it. Dig up the blade. Claim it! You're the true Scorcher."

Jesse looked at Smokey. His eyes were blazing. Saul juggled his own head. He then placed it back on his neck.

"It's not fun being dead, Jesse. Imagine that. And even though I'm only working with purgatory, I'm sure it's much better than whatever hell that Thing has in mind for us. Get to it, Jess! I know you got it in you!"

Saul disappeared right before the dog walker's eyes. Smokey licked Jesse's hand, then he ran into the snowy woods and vanished as well.

Jesse stood alone on the field. The sky was quickly darkening. He looked up as a blood moon rose, and it was accompanied by sinister stars. The dog walker felt dread, heavier than an iron casket sinking through quicksand. The Perseus constellation was above his head, but only Caput Algol, the Demon Star, blinked. Perseus and his sword were dull and lifeless. The head of Medusa leered down at Jesse, and it began to descend, bringing the dark sky with her. Jesse tried to scream again. He heard hissing all around him. He couldn't move. The dog walker was suddenly surrounded by black robed figures. One pulled back its hood. Jesse stared into Smith's arrogant, hateful face. He flicked his serpent tongue at the dog walker.

Jesse suddenly heard a woman's scream over the collective hissing. Claudia appeared next to Smith. She was held captive by a robed figure.

"Jesse, help!"

The sky was falling. The Demon Star was quickly dragging it down to crush the earth below. Some of the acolytes began to take off their hoods. The serpent-faced creatures gazed up in rapture at their impending doom. Jesse was finally able to scream. The forked tongue of the Gorgon was only

85

inches away from his face. He jolted out of bed, breathing heavily.

The room was pitch black. A chill wind rushed through the open window. Jesse caught his breath. He collected himself, then kicked out of his half-rolled blanket. Jesse stood. Moonlight poured into his bedroom. He walked toward his window and looked up at the stars. Nothing unusual. He glanced down into the backyard. There were only a few stray cats slinking around garbage cans.

Jesse wiped his eyes, then yawned heavily. It still didn't sound like his roommate was home. The apartment was dead quiet. The nightmare's details were beginning to slip away. His head felt clearer. Jesse sat down on his bed, and he thought about the earlier events of the day. They were distant and surreal.

Jesse hoped they stayed that way. He checked his watch. A little after 11 pm. For a moment he actually forced himself to believe that his entire day was just a part of that fading nightmare.

Jesse walked over to his desk. His legs ached. He turned his lamp on. The nightmare rushed back to him. He stared at the diary on his floor. It was wide open, the pages were no longer stuck together. A flash of Saul juggling his own head, telling Jesse that he had some kind of mission to fulfill. He forced the dream memory away.

"No. Nope. Fuck that!" Jesse quickly grabbed the diary off his floor. He wanted no part of it, yet he fought hard against the impulse to read the now revealed pages. Jesse tried to ignore the potent flow of electrical energy radiating from the thing. It completely took away the pain from his earlier fall. He hustled over to his window and hurled the diary into the night. It clanked off a garbage can lid and nearly hit an orange tabby. The cat hissed then bolted out of the alley. Jesse slammed the window closed. A fierce wind howled outside the old Brooklyn glass pane.

"I need air. I have to get the hell out of here and sort this out."

The dog walker put on a heavy green hoodie. He grabbed his satchel and left his bedroom.

The lights in the empty living room were on. He locked his door and looked at the large wooden table. Six chairs were pulled up around it, and an old school Dragon Lance campaign module was set up on top of it, stat charts, miniature figurines and rolling dice.

A gaming night, thought Jesse. So, Marvin had been here. He must have just stepped out, maybe to go on a snack run. Junk food was conspicuously absent from the large oak table. The weed wasn't, however. He could still smell Kush in the living room. Marvin might be back any minute, with his collection of gamer friends/drug addicts. Jesse had absolutely no interest in seeing any of them. He ran toward the front door, keys jangling loudly.

Jesse swung it open and stepped out into the empty hallway. He locked up and breezed down three flights, dashing out of the tenement. A cold draft, more winter than autumn, greeted him as he burst onto the sidewalk. The streetlight was off, and had been broken for the better part of a week now. Jesse stood in shadow. He decided to head toward Fifth Avenue. The dog walker strode past a closed barber shop and a corner bodega. There were all kinds of ghouls and goblins roaming the avenue. It was the night before Halloween after all, and some people were in costume. The Slope had long moved south. Transplants stepped casually through the working-class Latino community. There were all types of people out celebrating this pre-All Hallows' Eve. Jesse crossed the street. He suddenly heard Marvin talking loudly about the Pathfinder gaming system. Jesse glanced left and saw him walking along the avenue with an elf and wizard. He couldn't help but smile. They'd be dressed like this any given game night. They probably didn't even know tomorrow was Halloween. Jesse rushed out of their sight, heading south.

He decided to grab a drink at Uneeda Shot, his local   dive.

VIII
JESSE VENTURA GETS DRUNK
AND SPEAKS SPANISH

L ucy was tending bar. She smiled when Jesse walked in.

"Hi Jesse." He nodded while sitting down on a creaky stool. She took out two shot glasses and a bottle of tequila. Lucy was in her mid-twenties, a Korean American transplant from San Francisco. She had a Bettie Page thing going on, same hair style and make up. She quickly picked up on Jesse's mood.

"What's up? You ok?"

"Not   really."

"Free shots for Luke Dog Walker." She poured the tequila. They quickly tapped their glasses and drank. It burned his throat and shook him from the skull on down. It did make Jesse feel better, though. There was no doubting that. He stared at the pictures of random eighties era kitsch taped to the wall behind the bar. Mr. T scowled at Jesse, Gidget grinned, a poster of the film, *Return of the Living Dead*, and a picture of Linnea Quigley as Trash next to it. Lucy stood by the photo of that red-haired punk, dressed in a Dead Boy's band shirt and a tight leather mini skirt. She poured two more shots. They downed them. Jesse heard a loud shout from a pool table in the back. Lucy rolled her eyes.

"Got some serious Bros playing pool right now, Jesse. It's been pretty quiet but trust me, this is the calm before Buck Cherry. We're dealing with nostalgic, thirtysomething-year-old Brobots. I can feel a Dave Matthews storm brewing. If it rains I'm tossing on Creed. Fuck it. I'm all in." Jesse smiled faintly. Lucy frowned.

"Hard day at work?"

Jesse shrugged and looked around Uneeda Shot. The two grown frat boys clanged their cue balls around wildly at the back of the bar. A tall, slumped man wearing a beige flannel shirt sat alone at a table close to Lucy and Jesse. His back was turned.

"Strange day."

"Strange how?"

"Well..." Jesse decided there was no need to get into most of it. Just the basic stuff that wouldn't make him sound absolutely insane. He didn't want to get cut off too early. His plan was to get blackout drunk. Jesse wanted to completely wipe the day away. "One of my dogs got hit by a car."

"That's horrible! How did it—"

"Ventura! The Dog Walker! I knew I recognized your voice!" shouted the man at the table. Lucy stared at Jesse, confused. The dog walker recognized the man's voice, as well. It was Blake, Claudia's boyfriend. Blake turned to Jesse. His smile was plastic as Tupperware, his face doughy and unremarkable. There was a bit of blonde soul patch on his chin. His long hair was tied up in a man bun. Blake's signature black turtleneck hugged his scrawny neck.

Jesse glared at him, and said nothing.

"Have a quick drink with me. I'm on my way out. I have an early date with Claudia, as you probably already know! Right, homie?"

Blake's plastic smile didn't remotely come close to touching his eyes. Jesse felt like smacking him. The dog walker suddenly remembered his conversation with Victor. He also remembered the statue Blake had given Claudia as a gift. Something was up.

"I'll be back in a minute, Lucy." He left his drink and walked over to Blake's table.

He sat across from him. Blake was still smiling. Jesse wasn't. He nodded at Claudia's boyfriend. One of the pool players in the back stumbled past the two. "You want a drink, Jesse?"

"No. What's up, man? What do you want to speak to me about?"

"Photograph" by Nickelback suddenly started to play on the jukebox. A red-haired Brobot with a backwards Cleveland Cavaliers cap slapped his hands together, dancing past Jesse and Blake.

"Kroger!" he screamed, scampering back to his pool table.

Blake drank from his pint, never taking his eyes off Jesse. The dog walker stared at him with open contempt.

"Ahhh..." Blake moaned, putting his glass down. He smoothed his turtleneck with one quick motion, then he smiled again.

"Suit yourself. This Shock Top is a revelation, Jesse Ventura. By the way, I don't ever know if I told you but, um, great name."

Jesse continued to grill him.

"Jesse Ventura. Like the wrestler/politician/conspiracy theorist. You don't believe in conspiracies, do you Jesse Ventura? Kooky shit like cults and things that go bump in the night? How's your day been going?"

Jesse watched Blake watching him. He gave him nothing.

"You want to speak to me about a fucking wrestler? Really?"

Blake kept smiling, but the scrutinizing look in his eyes faded a bit. He suddenly laughed. The sound was shrill and obnoxious. Blake clapped his hands together and stomped his feet, shaking his head back and forth. He abruptly stopped.

"Ok. Let's shoot straight then. You hittin' it? You hittin' it? Ha-ha! You smashing or what, brother?"

He laughed again. Jesse glared at him.

"You hittin i— "

"What the hell are you talking about?"

Blake rolled his eyes. He shook his head incredulously and beat out a rhythm on the table.

"Claudia, homie! My babe! Are you fucking her?"

"Get the fuck out of this bar, man."

"Wait, wait, wait, just hear me out. Come on, man. Please. Just hear me out. Please, man!" Jesse glanced at Lucy. She was looking at Blake contemptuously.

"You ok, guy?" she asked.

"We're fine Lucy," said Jesse.

She shrugged, and continued to glance at the two as she wiped the bar down with a rag. Jesse stared hard at Blake.

"If you did at one point, I mean, just let me know. I understand, she's a hot bitch, I wouldn't be fucking her if she wasn't."

Jesse felt like slapping Blake for talking about his own girlfriend like that. He said nothing, though.

"But if you still are, I mean...I just need to know. I really need to determine her worth, you know, muchacho? I can't go around thinking I got the keys to an Aston Martin when it's really a 71' Ford Pinto! You see Jesse, she gets goofy when I bring you up. And those fucking stupid flea bags just *love* you. I mean listen; I can see it. You're an attractive guy. You got kind of a laid back, pot smokin', Matt McConaughey drifter thing going on. Am I right? That's your thing?"

"I think that turtleneck is cutting off the oxygen to your brain, man. What the fuck are you talking about?"

"I get it. I like *Dazed and Confused*, but I'm a much bigger fan of *Reality Bites*. And reality does bite for you, Jesse. You see, Jay-Z follows me on Instagram and Snapchat! I've snorted 8 balls with Leo! I have tons of clients, and I make unholy amounts of money. You see, Jesse? I'm a winner, and I don't get caught up. I just need to know what's up. I feel like there's something there between you and Claudia. And if that's true there could be some very serious consequences."

"You threatening me, dickhead?"

"No. But some things are out of my control. And it's not even about me. Or my feelings."

The expression on Blake's face darkened. He stared   at   Jesse   and   shrugged. "What does that even mean, Blake?"

Claudia's boyfriend rolled his eyes and slumped back against the chair. "Just tell me what's going on, man."

"No, Blake. I've never *hit that*.

Claudia's boyfriend laughed. He smiled elastically at the dog walker once again.

"Cause, I'm all about bros before hoes! I just ain't tryin' to be with no lyin' stank-ass ho. Nah' mean? Hell, ese, if the girl's a trick we can both hit that shit. You got a wrestler's last name. Little tag team action, maybe?"

"I'm done." Jesse stood. So did Blake. He put his jacket on and started walking toward the exit.

"I just gotta know if that punani is Cognac or Thunder Bird, Jesse the Dog Walker. And I gotta know one more thing. Do you love her?" He turned around to face Jesse. Blake watched his face intently. Jesse scowled and looked away. The dog walker didn't even realize that he had unconsciously nodded his head.

"I got my answer, then. Well, let's hope you're not the One." Blake's tone was cold and formal.

"Not the One? What? Which One?"

Blake was already striding past the bar. He tossed a twenty-dollar bill on it.

"His drink's on me," he said, walking toward the front door. Jesse ran after him. He grabbed Blake's shoulder and stopped him dead in his tracks. Blake turned around. He stared at Jesse blankly.

"You said if I'm the One? What are you talki—"

A slow grin spread across his face.

"The One? I mean her soul mate, muchacho! You don't wanna wife that up. The girl can't cook worth a shit. It's takeout every night with her."

"That's not what you meant."

He broke out of the dog walker's grasp. Jesse stared him up and down.

"What the fuck does Claudia see in you?"

"A future. Similar stock. Claudia and I are from the same world, Jesse. You're just not in our class. See you around dog walker," he said coldly, walking out of Uneeda Shot.

Jesse said nothing. He slowly walked back to his seat. Lucy stared at him.

"What the hell was that about?"

"Some client's boyfriend. He thinks I'm—"

"Are you?"

"No. He's just a dick."

"He was here since five. Fucking weird. The guy drank like twenty Shock Tops and never once used the bathroom. Creepy."

"Strange bladder. Stranger day. Let me get another shot. I want to forget *everything*."

Lucy poured him more tequila. He downed it.

"One of your dogs was hit by a car?" she asked heavily.

Jesse rubbed his hands through his hair. "I don't want to talk about that anymore. I just want to get plastered and forget this day ever happened. Can you help me out, Lucy?"

She smiled.

"Of course. As always."

"Can I get a Stella and another shot?"

He took a hundred-dollar bill out of his jacket, quickly handing it to Lucy. Jesse had nearly forgotten about the money he'd made today. There were clumps of it inside his satchel.

"Well look at you," she said flatly.

Jesse decided that he was going to spend all of Smith's cash tonight. It was filthy lucre, and it was burning a hole in his pocket.

"Shots are on the house!" screamed Jesse, as Chad Kroger continued to croon over the jukebox. He slammed another hundred down onto the bar. The Brobots stared up at him from their game of pool, confused.

"Free drinks!" shouted Lucy. The pool players cheered, then stormed the bar within seconds. The liquor helped take the edge off. Jesse spent the next hour forgetting the day and chatting with Lucy, while sporadically summoning the Brobots for their free drinks.

"Her name is what?"

97

"Her name is Chuleta! She's a Latweena dog walker," said Jesse drunkenly.

She smiled at him and nodded.

"Oh! You're talking about your book. You lost me there for a minute, buddy. I thought her name was Lizzie? What does chuleta mean?"

"Yeah! My book! I changed her fucking name! I think chuleta means pork chop!"

"You think?"

"Yeah! Rosie's boyfriend wants her to move to Colorado with him so they can grow weed together. But she doesn't want to."

"You Give Love a Bad Name" by Bon Jovi came on the jukebox. The frat boys cheered. So did Jesse. Lucy began to creep away from their conversation.

"But she doesn't want to go because Rosie loves her job!"

Lucy turned around. "It's Rosie, now? Um, ok. She's like you. You love walking dogs, too."

Jesse drunkenly shook his head.

"No not like me! Yeah! Maybe a little bit, yeah! Did I ever tell you I'm half— "

"Yeah. Yeah. Yeah. You've told me, Jesse."

"You give love Brad's name!" shouted the dog walker at the pool players, drunkenly butchering the song's lyrics. They shouted back the Ohio State Buckeyes Battle Cry. He stared at them and smiled.

"Told you what, Lucy?"

The bar was packed an hour later. Jesse ordered drinks for every single bar hopper who staggered into Uneeda Shot. The dog walker drank, flirted, played pool, and had inarticulate conversations with nearly everyone in the dive. Lucy decided to ditch the Jersey Shore playlist at around 3am. She threw it back to the nineties, blasting songs from Alanis Morissette's album, *Jagged Little Pill*. Jesse sang along. Two middle-aged Mexican mariachis wearing black sombreros and burgundy cowboy boots suddenly stumbled into the bar. They took one look around and were ready to dart back out, but Jesse screamed and stopped them. They almost dropped their guitar cases. Jesse attempted to speak Spanish.

"Amigos! Tequila! Muevate, entre...entre!"

He ran over to mariachis and motioned for them to stay. Jesse ordered them shots, and they thanked him in broken English. He thanked them in incorrect Spanish. They called him a kind gringo, and he made a toast for the country of Mexico as Alanis Morissette burned Dave Coulier.

"Amigos!" he yelled.

"Amigos!" they yelled back.

The room was beginning to seriously sway for Jesse after that last round. He promptly sat down on the bar stool closest to the exit.

He smiled drunkenly at everybody in Uneeda Shot. Frat boys wrestled with one another on the floor in front of a billiards table. It didn't stop the game, however. People were singing and hugging, others screwing each other loudly in the bathroom. Jesse loved it. It was like that scene in Gremlins, where all the monsters got drunk at the bar and fucked shit up.

Two women were making out with each other in a corner as Hootie & the Blowfish played on the jukebox. Brobots stared at them moronically, occasionally cheering them on. A black transwoman dressed like Ziggy Stardust stood by the bar, arguing with Lucy over her Betty Page look, and accusing her of cultural appropriation.

"I did this. I caused all this..." whispered Jesse. He was content.

The two mariachis took out their guitars. They looked at one another, then Jesse. He jumped up from his seat. The room tilted. Jesse nodded at them fervently.

"Cut the music, Lucy! Everybody! Hey everybody! Quiet!"

Lucy shut off the jukebox. The pool players stopped playing, the women stopped making out. The wrestlers still wrestled, but at a much quieter and more respectful level. Whoever was fucking in the bathroom kept it up, not paying Jesse any mind.

"Ladies and gentlemen, I give you the two amigos! Andela! Andela!"

The two mariachis nodded at one another. They began to passionately play "Guantanamera." Chants of "Viva La Mexico" began halfway through the song, and when they were done everybody broke out into a loud drunken cheer. "Now this is my America!" Jesse said to Lucy, flashing her a thumbs up and a drunken smile.

Lucy shrugged, then gave the transwoman she'd been arguing with a dirty look. She plugged in the jukebox again. AC/DC blared. The musicians put their guitars away. They sat down and ordered more shots of tequila. They drank slowly, in moody silence, while staring down at the bar counter. Jesse imitated them, blocking out the rest of Uneeda Shot. He suddenly felt the events of the day slithering back into his mind.

Jesse ordered another beer. Lucy brought him a tall glass of water.

He drank it quickly and sat in silence, exhausted. Jesse fought back the memories.

The dull blur of the alcohol still dominated, and he was thankful for that at the very least. The crowd in the bar, seeing that no free drinks had been ordered for them in over twenty minutes, grew bored and began to trickle out of the dive, not bothering to thank Jesse or the two musicians for his money and their music.

The Dead Kennedys replaced Guns N' Roses on the jukebox.

Jesse looked around. The mariachis continued to sulk and drink quietly. Lucy mopped vomit off the floor. The two original Brobots were still playing pool in the back. The dive's front door was suddenly pushed open. Smokey the Husky trotted in. Jesse stared vacantly at his dead dog. The Husky sat down on his haunches. He gazed at Jesse, blue and brown eyes shining brightly.

"Smokey?"

The dog barked. Nobody paid it any mind. Jesse turned away. He tapped the mariachi sitting next to him.

"Look!" Jesse shouted. The mariachi stared at him. Jesse pointed to Smokey.

The musician looked over his shoulder. He shrugged, then shook his head at Jesse, confused. Smokey howled again.

"The dog! You see it, amigo?"

Silence. The mariachi continued to stare at him, puzzled. "¿Qué quieres, gringo estúpido? ¿Por qué no hablas español? Parece hispano."

"Trabajo!" Jesse shouted, drunkenly confusing the word "dog" in Spanish with the word "work."

"Trabajo?" the mariachi asked quizzically.

Jesse shook his head in frustration. He looked back at the spectral dog. It continued to stare at him ruefully. Jesse faced the mariachi again.

"My dead dog is staring at us."

The mariachi shrugged. He nervously offered Jesse his glass of tequila. The dog howled. Jesse frowned and covered his ears. The mariachi stared at him in complete bewilderment. Smokey stopped howling. He trotted out the door and back into the dark streets.

"Trabajo!"

"Trabajo? Ofrendamos trabajo?"

"Trabajo! Yes! Si!"

Jesse bolted up from the bar stool, head spinning. He steadied himself, then ran out of Uneeda Shot. The mariachi next to him jumped up as well, lost in the moment and overcome with confusion and excitement. He smashed his shot glass on the floor.

His friend woke up and screamed wildly. He threw his shot glass at the picture of Mr. T on the bar wall. The mariachi missed badly, and it winded up hitting Gidget.

"What the fuck!!!" screamed Lucy, as she dropped her vomit covered mop.

Both men strapped their guitars across their backs.

"Trabajo!" shouted the first mariachi as he bolted out the door. His friend followed.

Jesse ran hard after his dead dog as it dashed toward First Avenue. He heard sudden shouts from behind. The two mariachis were running after him.

"What the fuck!"

"Trabajo!" the one closest to him screamed.

"Yes!" Jesse shouted. "This way!"

The dog walker watched Smokey turn left around the corner, onto First Avenue. He followed. The Husky pulled up in front of a building, then turned to face Jesse. Smokey howled. Jesse tripped on a rubber snake mask and fell to the ground hard. The world spun violently. The mariachis stopped running. They looked around the desolate area, then at one another. Smokey darted across the street. He vanished into darkness. Jesse threw up.

They mariachis stared at him, and shook their heads. They walked in front of the bland-looking building Smokey had been standing in front of only moments before.

Jesse's head was spinning. He closed his eyes. A mariachi knocked on the building's front door. It swung open instantly. Dozens of hands reached out to yank the two men inside. A mariachi's sombrero flew off and landed on the pavement. The door slammed shut.

Jesse opened his eyes. The world stopped spinning. He managed to stand. Jesse wiped his mouth and stepped away from his waste. He blinked hard, then squinted while looking across the street. Jesse couldn't see much beyond the orange glow of the streetlamp. "Smokey," he slurred. Jesse fought the sudden urge to vomit again. He looked down and picked up the rubber snake mask.

Your friend will guide you to their snake pit.

Shards of the dream flashed through his mind. Brilliant and glittering, miniscule and fragmented.

Stop them before they know it's you. Kill their leader.

Jesse shook his head in confusion. He once again peered into the darkness across the street.

"Come back, Smokey," he mumbled.

The dog walker suddenly heard muted laughter and music coming from the building to his left. He crept toward it. It was a seedy looking strip club named The Diamondback. He stared at its tinted windows and heavy metal door. It didn't seem to be open for business, and looked as if it hadn't been for years. Still, he could hear music and voices inside, behind that iron tank of a door.

He saw the mariachi's black sombrero lying in front of the entrance. Jesse stared at it, afraid, in spite of the massive amounts of liquid courage coursing through his system. The image of Saul casually juggling his own head flashed across the dog walker's mind.

Kill their leader.

"Amigos," whispered Jesse. He suddenly yearned for the comforting warmth of the diary in his breast pocket. Jesse put on the snake mask, and he approached the door. He tested its knob. It wouldn't budge. He was about to knock when a speakeasy grate opened in the hunk of metal. Two cold, gray eyes peered out at him from the Judas window.

"Password," said the deep voice.

Jesse stood in dumb silence.

"Password," the voice repeated, angry and dangerous.

It came to the dog walker in a flash. He remembered the monster Trevor John screaming those strange words.

"Caput Algol."

The grate closed. The door swung open.

"Welcome," said a tall, bicep-swollen bouncer. He was dressed like Baby Huey from the neck down. A red ceramic serpent mask covered his face.

Jesse Ventura stepped inside the snake pit.

IX
BACCHANAL IN THE SNAKE PIT,
THE BILLY OCEAN INFERNO

The inside of the strip club was unlike anything Jesse would have ever imagined. It was clean and warm, and if it wasn't for the elevated wooden stage with the stripper pole in its center you would think you were at some lounge in Park Slope. The bouncer slammed the front door and locked it. He sat down on a stool, quickly taking out a cell phone from the back of his diaper. He gazed down at the screen, oblivious to the world around him.

"What the fuck kind of strip club is this?" Jesse muttered.

The place had a large amount of people in it, at least thirty. Jesse could tell what kind of people they were despite their masks and costumes. They were not the type of people you would expect to see hanging out at a titty bar on First Avenue at 5 o'clock in the morning.

Urban professionals sat on plush couches, drinking Belgian lager from mason jars. They chatted and laughed amicably with one another as

"In the Neighborhood" by Tom Waits played over the sound system. There was a large wooden bar off to Jesse's left side. Masked couples spoke quietly to one another on bar stools. No one even bothered to look in Jesse's direction. Past the bar was a lounge, where most of the patrons were gathered on sofas and chairs. They were seated in front of the stage and pole. A large, red velvet curtain separated the platform from the staging area at the back of the club.

Jesse watched snake-mask-wearing mothers with baby strollers seated around the stage, knitting ankle-high socks while drinking from bottles of craft beer. The baby carriages were ignored.

"What the fuck is this?" he whispered to himself, "Is this a new Tea Lounge?"

He stumbled over to an empty bar stool. A skinny man with a massive beard approached him. He was the only person not wearing a mask. Jesse recognized him instantly. He was the guy who had been setting up the display mannequins at American Apparel earlier in the day—the weirdo who laid down next to them while he gazed at Ginger and Jesse.

He smiled at the dog walker.

"Hey. What's going on, man? What do you need?" His accent was Californian.

Jesse stared at him blankly. He pulled the top of his green hood down, covering more of his mask. Jesse violently yanked the satchel strap away from his throat, and his bag nearly careened into a pair of vodka bottles on the bar counter. The bartender didn't drop his smile.

"What's going on, man?" asked the bearded one.

"Little bit of this. Little bit of that?" Jesse stammered   drunkenly. The bartender's smile widened.

"Ahhhhh...got you," he said cheerfully.

Jesse squinted hard at him. He looked over his shoulder at the brawny bouncer. The Bicepasaurus was still looking down at his cell phone.

"You *got* me?" Jesse asked darkly.

The bartender shrugged. Then chuckled.

"I got you, man. I'm sayin' I got you. Ya know? Anyway— "

"Where did the two mariachis go? They came in here a few minutes ago. They're my amigos. Have you seen them?"

The bartender shook his head. His smile faltered a bit. "Can't say I have, my man."

"You had to see them. One guy had a sombrero on his head. They both had guitars on their backs."

"We don't let people like that in here, man. Unless they work for us. Sorry. Would you like some sparkling apple cider?" Jesse shook his head.

This guy is a fucking idiot, thought the dog walker.

The bartender shrugged and looked at the empty stage. A couple of indeterminate gender were making out three stools away from Jesse, the bottom halves of their snake masks pulled up. They were sitting next to a tall man wearing a black robe, and an extremely ornate cobra mask. It was gold trimmed, and embedded with diamonds. The man was bouncing a dwarf dressed in a tiger outfit on his lap. The little person, like everyone else except the bartender, was wearing a snake mask.

They both turned to face the couple, and the dwarf jumped off the cobra man's lap. He started grinding against the horny couple. They smiled. The bartender walked over to the little person and high fived him.

"My big cousin right here is going to tear you two a new one," said the bartender, grinning. The couple nodded their heads enthusiastically. The dwarf gave them a lap dance.

"Oh man," Jesse muttered.

The bartender strutted back to the dog walker.

"You sure you don't want anything to drink, my man?"

"No, no. I'm— "

"Well, enjoy the festivities! They're about to begin! We're going to find out what's what!" He ran over to the other side of the bar and grabbed his phone. The bartender shut Tom Waits off in mid-grumble. Strange, ethereal music began to play. It sounded vaguely Middle Eastern, but not quite. Jesse couldn't identify any of the instruments being played, couldn't in fact tell if they were instruments at all. They sounded like voices imitating the howling wind.

Mason jars and glass cups began to clank down on the hard surfaces of bar and table. Everyone dropped what they were doing. Mothers stopped knitting, couples stopped chatting. A certain dwarf stopped grinding. They watched the empty stage. The red velvet curtain began to part. Nobody stepped out, but the eyes of the audience remained glued to the platform. Jesse looked over his shoulder. Brolic Baby Huey was watching, as well. The weird music was making Jesse's mind hazy. He could hear a voice in it. A chant.

Caput Algol.

Some of the masked patrons began to repeat the words. Jesse suddenly smelled a pungent incense coming from the direction of the stage. A figure stepped out from behind the parted curtains. The lights above the stage brightened. Some audience members gasped, while others emitted jubilant squeals of excitement. The olive-skinned woman was nude, except for a long black

111

veil that covered her face and the tops of her shoulders. She was voluptuous. A tattoo of a red serpent twisted around her body, its vivid coils etched beneath her giant breasts, slim waist and powerful thighs. Its tail tapered off by her left heel. Jesse had seen her before. It was the woman who had been jogging with Smith. She stared down at the floor.

The crowd went silent. The woman onstage glided forward, never taking her eyes off the floor. She touched the pole with her right forefinger, and left it there. The audience began to chant loudly once again, nearly drowning out the sound system.

Caput Algol...Caput Algol...

Jesse felt the hypnotic effect of the chant and the strange woman onstage. He couldn't look away, couldn't get off his bar stool. Jesse was trapped in this snake pit.

Kill the leader.

A plump man wearing a purple snake mask and a lime green cardigan was sitting at the other end of the bar, and he was really losing it. He was screaming the chant at the top of his lungs in a thin, nasally voice, while making clawing motions at the stage. His delirious holler only increased when the second figure appeared onstage. The fat man in the lime green cardigan violently pounded his fists on the bar. He was frothing at the mouth.

Jesse shook his head and looked away from the stage, trance broken. He'd recognize that cock anywhere. Trevor John.

He was nude except for a wooden serpent's mask, and his giant wart-covered schlong was erect and pointed at the audience.

The monster held a black satin bag in one hand above his head. He held a small bronze headdress of twisting serpents in the other. Their eyes were diamonds, their forked tongues gold. He stood beside the woman wearing the black veil. She looked up from the floor.

Trevor John placed the crown on her head.

She received a thunderous round of applause.

The fat guy in the lime green cardigan completely lost it. He squealed, " Caput Algol" with a berserk urgency, and he rushed the stage, ripping his cardigan off. A stroller mom dressed like Dorothy from the Wizard of Oz and a guy wearing a Wilco t-shirt jumped up from a black couch. They tried to restrain the fat man as he groped at Trevor John's member. They held him back, while fondling his sweaty man-breasts. Still, the three continued to chant in unison, never taking their eyes off the two figures onstage.

The woman took her finger off the pole and raised it over her head. The bartender ran to his phone, and he almost tripped. He cut the music. The crowd stopped chanting. Trevor John continued to hold the bag above his head. The woman kept her finger up in the air.

"The time draws near. Caput Algol!" she suddenly screamed.

The audience cheered insanely. They screamed "Caput Algol" back at her.

"Caput Algol!" bellowed Trevor John.

The man in the ornate cobra mask seated by the bar suddenly stood and walked toward the stage. The crowd fell silent, they parted for him. He stopped and stood before the audience, below the naked woman.

Smith ripped off his mask. He gazed at his acolytes.

Jesse felt a surge of anger. A missed opportunity. He drunkenly looked around the bar for a weapon. Nothing. He felt the Zippo in his pocket, and Jesse realized he had lighter fluid in his bag. He took it out. Jesse glanced at the two bottles of 100 Absolut a few inches away. The bartender's dish rag was crumpled next to the vodka bottles. Jesse had an idea. The bouncer was standing several feet in front of him. The dog walker would have to time it right, but there was a chance. The chant started up again. Jesse looked at the stage.

The woman took off her veil. Her eyes were huge and frightening, an unnatural bright green. The crowd moaned and screamed in excitement.

"Algol Egregor! This woman will soon be the vessel of our goddess! The shade of Algol, Ra's al-Ghul, the great constellation of Immortal Knowledge, who will destroy this coil and give us new skin so we may live forever in her starry wisdom! Along the warm scales of her eternal power! Caput Algol!" Smith screamed.

The masked acolytes chanted back fervently.

"Give us knowledge Great Star, of which Lilith is just one shade! The Gorgon we worship another! Tseih She Ke, Exhalation of the Piled-Up Corpses! Caput Algol! Ra's al-Ghul!"

Jesse crept off his bar stool. He grabbed the two bottles of vodka and the rag. The bartender and bouncer paid him no mind. They were too immersed in the ritual. Jesse doused the rag in alcohol and lighter fluid. He stuffed it in one of the bottles, and waited.

"Dark Mother! We will destroy the Light in your name...Sirius! So we may be reborn in your dead heat! Give us True Knowledge of your Enemy. Champion of the Summer Star, whose inhumane light gives hope to the doomed and the foolish! Who now holds the badge, Ishum? Who is the newly anointed? Who would wield the ancient blade, Erra? Who is the Scorcher?"

"Ventura!" shouted someone in the audience. Jesse recoiled, and nearly dropped the bottle. He saw Trevor John, who was still holding the bag over his head, nod wildly in agreement.

"It is not for us to say! Our dark goddess must speak! May she speak through the voice of the Pretender, the enemy's false harbinger!" The woman wearing the crown of serpents hissed. Trevor John lowered the bag. He took a severed head out of it.

"Saul." said Jesse heavily.

Trevor John held the head of Jesse's mentor and friend out in front of the audience.

They screamed and cursed.

"In this hour, when the Veil is thin, this early morning before the meteor's passing, before our Great Conjunction, we implore you to speak through the mouth of this false harbinger. Caput Algol! Tell us the true identity of the Scorcher!"

Silence. Jesse began spilling liquor and lighter fluid onto the counter. There was the sudden sound of fabric being ripped in half. Nearly everyone looked at one another in alarm, except for Smith and the two onstage. They were calm, and completely in control. Saul's decapitated head began to shake. There were gasps from the masked cult members.

Saul Cohen's eyes opened. And so did his mouth. He spoke in a voice that was not his own. The words boomed. They were understood clearly.

"Jesse Ventura!" it screamed in a deep bellow.

The acolytes went berserk. Shouting, cursing...

He was the one! We had him! We let him go! Kill him!

"Quiet!" yelled Smith. He stared around wildly, and there was a look of fear in his eyes. It quickly faded.

Saul's slowly blinked, then grinned.

"He must be sacrificed! And the one he loves must be killed!" screamed the demonic voice from Saul's decapitated head.

The one I love? thought Jesse.

"Claudia Summers must die!!" screamed Smith.

"What the fuck?" Jesse muttered. He flicked the Zippo, watching the liquor spread all the way down the bar. Only Jesse and the bouncer remained outside of the lounge area, and the bouncer was very close to it. He remained fixated on the grotesque spectacle.

The crowd went silent. Saul's face went still. Trevor John suddenly spiked the dead dog walker's skull onto the floor.

"Now submit your offerings to our mother! Submit them now! She has spoken to us, on the night before her incarnation!" Smith took off his robe, and he stood naked in front of the stage. Trevor John grabbed him by the back of his waist, and he gently lifted Smith up onto the wooden platform.

"Submit your offerings to our mother!"

The crowd began to rip their costumes off, but not their masks. The stroller moms began taking corpses of dead animals out of their baby carriages: small dogs, cats, raccoons. They tossed them at the feet of the woman onstage. Jesse watched in horror as one of the mariachi's bodies was tossed up onto the platform. The bearded bartender, who had gotten completely naked within the blink of an eye, picked up his phone.

"Caribbean Queen" by Billy Ocean began to play. He then bolted toward the stage. Jesse stared in shock and disgust as the naked revelers streamed onto the platform. They swarmed over the three, pulling them down toward the corpse-covered floor in a cacophony of orgiastic moans. Jesse stood and lit the Molotov cocktail.

"It's him! The dog walker!" screamed the dwarf in the tiger suit. He popped out from behind a bar stool. Jesse quickly kicked him against a wall.

The dog walker set the bar on fire, and then he tossed the Molotov cocktail at the stage. It exploded on top of a threesome. Screams of agony tore through the Diamondback. Jesse could somehow feel himself inside the flames, and he fanned them with his mind. The blaze quickly became an inferno.

The smoke spread rapidly, but Jesse could make out people escaping through the back. The naked bouncer was trying to rush Jesse, but the fire was already too intense. There was a solid buffer of flame between him and the members of Algol Egregor.

"Ventura!" screamed Trevor John from the burning stage. He stood motionless and unmasked amidst the flames, and he grinned savagely at Jesse. The dog walker froze. Trevor John bellowed as he ripped the stripper's pole out of the floor with one hand. He hurled it like a javelin at Jesse.

"Holy shit!" screamed the dog walker.

The bouncer accidentally stepped in front of the flying pole. It tore through the back of his skull and out the front of his face. His body tumbled into the wall of flames. Jesse screamed. Trevor John disappeared.

Jesse unlocked the heavy front door and swung it open. A cascade of smoke poured out into the cold street, along with Billy Ocean's upbeat melody. Jesse stepped out...and was then quickly pulled back in by his satchel.

"Motherfucker!!!!" screamed the burning dwarf as he struggled to yank Jesse back inside the strip club. Jesse kicked him hard, and he crashed into the bar. The dwarf held onto his satchel, however. Jesse's cash and wallet went up in flames. The dog walker then kicked the steel door closed.

The cold wind made Jesse's bones rattle. The streets were as empty and forbidding as they had been before. The black sombrero still lay on the asphalt. Jesse placed it on his head, then bolted away from the Diamondback. Adrenalin overtook his inebriation. Jesse ran hard. He could still hear the screams of Algol Egregor from over his shoulder. He could also hear vehicles rushing toward the scene. Oddly, he heard no ambulance or police sirens.

"Fuck!"

Jesse drunkenly tripped over his own feet. He fell hard on his face, next to a garbage can. Jesse ripped off the mask, groaning in agony. His face was hot with pain; it was so strong that it broke through the adrenalin and liquor haze. The world was a dark blur. He squinted and looked around, eyesight slowly coming back into focus. The inside of the mask was bloody. He threw it away. His nose was bleeding but not broken, he spat out a tooth. Jesse stood. He heard a loud explosion. It was the Diamondback. Jesse picked up the sombrero, and he placed it back on his head. The dog walker forced himself forward. Going home wasn't an option. His clients knew that address. Jesse would have to go somewhere else.

The Den.

Hopefully he would be safe there, at least for a little while. It was about ten blocks away, and two avenues up. He ran. Jesse's heart was beating overtime, a new rush of adrenalin spiked through his system. There was something else leading Jesse on, as well. Smokey was running beside him.

Jesse fought the pain, jogging as quickly as he could up the next ten blocks. The sun was beginning to rise, and that comforted him a bit. Smokey's phantasm vanished with the light.

He ran north when he got to Fifty-Sixth Street, up from desolate First and Second Avenue, and onto Third. Jesse got onto his block, ran to the front of his building. He looked around suspiciously, but saw no one. His green hoodie was covered in blood, his face was in agony. The dead mariachi's sombrero hugged his head tightly. Jesse opened the unlocked door of the apartment building, and thanked God that he didn't run into any tenants as he pulled himself up five flights of stairs.

For a moment he felt a sharp pang of fear as he looked for his keys and found only lint. Jesse checked the inside of his hoodie. They were there. The dog walker spilled in through the Den. Drunk, bloody, and exhausted. He closed the door as quietly as he could, then he stumbled through the empty living room. It was much larger than the living room in his apartment, more like a motel lobby. Still, the smell of cigarette smoke and pot lingered. TSR rulebooks along with fantastical miniatures and game dice sat on the large Ikea table. Had Marvin been here as well, last night? No sign of him or any other tenants now, however. The Den was still.

Jesse slumped into the bathroom and looked at himself in its mirror. He cringed. His face was bloody and already bruising. He was missing the tooth next to his front right. Jesse grabbed some Tylenol from the cupboard, then he turned on the faucet. He cupped the water with his right hand and swallowed the three pills quickly. Jesse washed most of the blood off his face. He stumbled out of the bathroom without shutting off the water. Jesse unlocked his room and staggered inside. The set up was sparse: a bed, locker, table and chair, and a window with no fire escape.

He swung the door shut and fell on top of his bed. Jesse kicked off his sneakers and got into a fetal position, pulling the thin blanket up over his sombrero-covered head. He went unconscious instantly, exhaustion dragging him down toward the   depths   of   sleep.

X
MARVIN TROUT THE DUNGEON MASTER
WAKES JESSE IN THE DEN

"**A**rise!"

The dog walker bolted up out of bed. He kicked his scraggly blanket onto the floor, and held his flat pillow in front of his chest like a shield. The sombrero was still on his head.

"What the fuck happened to your face!?!" screamed Marvin Trout.

The dog walker stared at the man. His white hair was shoulder length, and most of it was covered by a black hood. The golden makeup on his face was cracked and smeared. He gazed at Jesse with hourglass eyes. They had a golden hue, as well. Contacts. Trout was still in costume from the night before. What had started off as a traditional Dragonlance table top campaign had quickly escalated into a drug inspired Live Action Role Playing Game session. The companions of the Lance had LARPed long and hard.

"What the hell, Marvin?! Get out!" yelled Jesse, slurring his words.

He grasped for his blanket and found nothing but air. Jesse put the pillow over his face and lay down again. Marvin pulled back the window curtain. Bright sunlight drifted into the room. Jesse curled into a tight ball on his bare mattress. Marvin took a small joint and lighter out of his black robe's pocket. He lit up, then toked hard.

"Hey, Jess. You left the bathroom faucet on," said Trout in his southern accent. Jesse groaned miserably.

"I think you need to go to the hospital. You look fuckin' wrecked. And, um, why you wearin' that sombrero?"

Jesse ignored him. Marvin kicked his roommate's bed. Jesse popped his head out from underneath the pillow.

"What's wrong with you? Why are you here, Marvin?" The dog walker sat up. His head was pounding, and his body ached. The horrible memories from the previous day attempted to form in his mind. Jesse did his best to shut them out. They hammered against his skull, more severe than any migraine.

Jesse stood up on wobbly legs. He gazed into his roommate's golden face. "Your door was open, Jess. And you was screaming like you was getting murdered. You woke me and Amy up. You lucky my elf ranger from Bushwick don't have her 'lawful evil alignment' goin' on. It ain't that time of the month. She would have stuck a goddamned butter knife through your head."

"You were back at our apartment last night. I saw everything set up in the living room."

"Yeah. I was there for a little while."

"What are you doing here?" Jesse asked, suddenly suspicious. There was no telling who was who anymore.

"We finished the campaign. Real throwback. DL 16. World of Krynn. Shroomin,' smokin'. We were *in* fucking Dargaard Keep, man. We were all excited and pretty fucking high, so we got to LARPin'. We trooped out to the Den and finished up on the roof."

Marvin stared at him blankly. The dog walker sat back down on the edge of his bed. He suddenly yawned and wiped his eyes. *That sounds about right*, thought Jesse. On any given night you could spot the Dungeon Master and his band of drug addicted LARPers traveling along the desolate, industrial sections of Sunset Park and Industry City. Jesse knew he wasn't lying.

The dog walker stared at his odd roommate. He was in his late twenties: tall and thin, with a sharp hooked nose and eyes like a startled owl. Marvin Trout was a Republican gun nut from Georgia, and a lifelong dungeon master and drug dealer. His shitty part-time stock position at a rug store was a

125

cover, he always seemed to have tons of money. Jesse suspected his roommate was moving a lot more weight than he let on. Pounds, not ounces. He wasn't just a nickel and dime bagger, and he didn't move to New York to 'fall in love at Central Park,' like he so often claimed.

Jesse was also pretty sure he had an arsenal of illegal weapons hidden in their communal space, along with a good amount of his drugs. Marvin was using the Den as his stash house. His LARPing adventures were mainly a front for his drug operation, and most of his role-playing buddies were actually his associates. Jesse didn't ask him what was up. Marvin always paid his rent two months in advance, and he covered all the utility bills. Besides, Jesse bought his weed from Trout. Pure Hydro and Kush at a deep discount.

"Sorry about the faucet. And the random screaming." Jesse rubbed his temples. Marvin took another deep pull off the joint. He then held it out to his roommate.

"You want? Looks like you could use some."

Jesse took the joint and pulled hard. "So, what's the story, man? You get fucked up or somethin'? Why you wearin' that on your head? You decide to go Midnight Cowboy all of a sudden?"

Jesse shook his head, then took a few more deep tokes. He didn't say anything as he handed the joint back to Marvin. Fear and a deep sadness welled up in Jesse. He held back tears. "I'm going through some crazy shit, Marvin."

Silence. Some of the memories hammered through the dog walker's skull. Horrific screen shots from a snuff film he'd only narrowly escaped. Most of the memories were drowned out by the night's long river of alcohol consumption. Jesse hoped it stayed that way, even though he knew it wouldn't.

"You wanna talk about it? Is it serious? You need protection?"

"I don't know, man. I don't remember all that much, and what I do remember, well...it's just too weird and fucked up to talk about at this point."

Marvin tilted his wigged head. The black hood slipped off.

"You know where I'm at if you need to talk to me. You look fuckin' wrecked. You may want to consider going to the hospital, man." Marvin Trout toked the joint again. The dog walker suddenly felt something besides pain and confusion. It was a magnetic pull. A familiar feeling. It made the pit of his stomach quake with fear and anticipation, and it came from the drug dealing LARPer standing right before him.

"Why the hell you lookin' at me like that, Jesse?"

It was the diary. Marvin had it. Jesse looked at Trout's robed pockets. He could see the diary's outline in one. Jesse didn't remember everything about last night, but he did remember tossing the diary out of his window and into the garbage.

"What you got in your pocket?"

"Excuse you?"

"Did you find a Moleskine diary in our alleyway?"

Marvin took another puff from his joint. He slowly nodded his head up and down.

"Yep. How do you know? It belong to you? Figures. It's weird as shit." Marvin clipped the joint and put it behind his ear. He took out the book. It was filthy, and looked even more corroded now. More organic somehow, as if the cover was made out of green, decomposing tree bark. Only a few pages remained. The journal was transforming into something else. The dog walker instantly thought of a caterpillar in chrysalis.

The magnetic pull was definitely still there for Jesse.

"I found it in Prospect Park yesterday," Jesse said flatly.

"Why did you toss it?"

Jesse scratched the side of his face.

"It must have fallen out of my pocket."

Marvin opened the diary, thumbing through its dozen or so remaining pages.

"Out of your pocket and into a garbage can?"

"Yeah. The book had more pages before. What happened?"

Marvin ran his hand over the edges of the thing. He looked up at Jesse, who was staring at him uneasily.

"I found it like this. Just as it is. All gnarly and shit."

"And you're able to touch it?"

Marvin stared at him blankly.

"Yeah. Why wouldn't I be able to touch it? "

Jesse shrugged. Even though he consciously wanted no part of the thing he still felt possessive over it. Marvin must have read his mind, because he suddenly tried to hand it to Jesse.

"Do you...um, want your precious, back?"

There was an awkward silence as Jesse gazed at the diary. He suddenly yanked it out of Marvin's hand. The dog walker placed it on his lap.

"Whoever wrote in it is crazy, if it ain't meant to be fiction. All that shit about cults, and demon stars and being followed and sacrificed. It's fuckin' wonky, Jesse. Schizo shit."

"You were able to make out the writing?"

"Yeah. Some. Not all that much, though. You ain't read it?"

"Some. Not all that much."

"I think different people may have wrote different sections. You can see traces of other people's writin'. Like sentences in invisible ink that show themselves in different kinds of light. Some of it don't even look English. I think you smoked too much of my bud and wrote all this shit, Jesse. Just fess up. Be honest with me."

"I didn't write it," said the dog walker heavily. But he knew who did, in part. Jesse saw a flash of his mentor's severed head. He shook his own.

"Probably all just bullshit, anyhow. I doubt some guy broke into that Quaker cemetery in Prospect Park so he could bury a sword."

"Sword? You know about the sword?"

"I think you really should get to a hospital. You might have a concussion."

"I'm fine."

"I just told you I couldn't read everything. Just a few pages. But yeah. Guy was talkin' about some sword buried up in Friends' Cemetery."

Jesse nodded. The blade. He remembered parts of yesterday's dream.

"What time is it?" Jesse abruptly asked.

"Almost noon. I got some business to handle at two. I'm comin' back here later, though. Halloween party tonight. Strict 80's playlist baby, Ray Parker and Goblin is gettin' some love tonight."

"Did you hear anything about a building getting set on fire a few blocks away from here?"

Marvin shrugged. He grilled his roommate.

"No. Should I have?"

Jesse said nothing.

"You look horrible and sound even worse. Go see a doctor. For real, man."

"I feel better than I look," Jesse said, lying.

"Ok. Well, I lit you up for free and encouraged you to go to the hospital. That's my good deed for the year. I still have company, so please try and stifle the night terrors if you find yourself driftin' back into oblivion. Be quiet. Amy needs her rest."

Marvin left Jesse's room. He slammed the door behind him.

CHAPTER XI
THE DIARY ENTRY

Jesse opened the diary, and felt an electric pulse stream through his palm. The words practically jumped off the strange, fleshy parchment. The last few pages were all Saul. Jesse put the thing down on his bed. He thought about Claudia. They knew about her, and they wanted to hurt her because they knew that would hurt Jesse.

The dog walker couldn't piece it all together. He was having trouble distinguishing between reality and fantasy, actual memory and dream memory. Jesse feared he was losing his mind.

He staggered around the room, looking for his phone. His carrier bag. His wallet. Jesse couldn't find anything. He remembered that he broke his phone up on the hill where this all started. But where was everything else?

A flash of Smokey leading him through the dark streets.

He sat down on the bed again, trying to evaluate the situation as best he could. No cash. Credit cards and ATM card gone. No photo I.D. Claudia would already be upstate with the Chow Chow brothers and that shady fucker, Blake. No longer in Park Slope, and probably not safe with Blake. At least she wasn't in Brooklyn now, though. As for his own safety?

I'm fucked, thought Jesse. *I'm in way over my head.* He felt nauseous. Jesse picked up the diary again. Poor Saul, he thought. He read the last few pages.

I can't keep dodging them. Algol Egregor is relentless. I don't even think I'm safe in the cemetery anymore. They stalk me through the eyes of serpents, and I think some even know how to manipulate shadow and certain reflective surfaces. I abandoned my house on Ocean Parkway a year ago, and they burned down my home in Westchester a few months back. I'm sure the cabin in the Ozarks is safe, because it's where I dug up Erra. It's a sacred space. Still, I know I can't get there. They got me cornered, there's no real chance of getting out of Brooklyn alive. None of my people know where I'm at, and I prefer it that way. I don't want to get them involved, and I thank God I never had a wife and kids. I miss my dogs, but the Good Star has been sending strays to watch over me. I don't know how long that's going to last, though.

I'm completely off the grid.

They tried to grab me up at the Holiday Inn in Nassau two months ago, but I got away. They won't kill me yet, I think. They know I'm not the One. They want me to lead them to the real Scorcher. They want me to lead them to you.

The Quaker cemetery in Prospect Park has been a sanctuary for me. They have trouble detecting me here, and they can't set foot in it. I think some of them may not even be able to actually see the cemetery; it's an odd spiritual and physical blind spot for Algol Egregor.

I'm sure it's because the body of one of the star's harbingers is at rest here. That's why this thing disguised as a book led me to Friend's Cemetery, after it guided me to the Ozarks, and Erra. I'm too much of a coward to wield the blade. I bit off more than I could chew, you see. They can draw me out through their sorcery, even though they can't come inside. Everyday their pull gets stronger.

Sirius doesn't give me enough strength.

Understand this, Scorcher: those fixed stars above our heads are not lifeless. Those constellations are the repositories of vast spiritual powers beyond our wildest imagination. They are entities. Stellar Oversouls, sentient and powerful. Everything in their system, from the largest planet to the smallest beam of starlight, is just a minute reflection of their Greater Consciousness. The alien life forms in them, if they have any, are also subservient to their will.

But those Great Stars also have to follow a Greater Cosmic Law, and so must we. They help to create the raw dream stuff we mold our deities out of, and in exchange we let them live and die through us. They don't know death like we know it, you see. We have the ability to push past oblivion, to travel to the greater Multiverse beyond. Our particular solar system is a vehicle to the First Source. Our way of dying is unique in that regard. Our solar system's passageway to parallel threads beyond the physical universe is manufactured, in part, by the dreams those undying stars provide us.

But they're trapped.

They can't die the way we can. They can power our dreams, enter and influence them, but they can never truly inhabit that state without us. And there's no real access to the worlds beyond death without the ability to dream. They can't leave this strand of the multiverse. That's our system's spiritual legacy, in this galaxy, at the very least. Most stellar Oversouls accept this. Some don't. Some want to see us destroyed. The travelers that pass through this system, and all systems, asteroids both major and minor, are operatives of our universe's Greater Principle.

Some can be corrupted, and one has.

It's going to align with the Demons Star, and a physical manifestation of an entire solar system

135

will then be incarnated onto our planet. Ishum has informed me that this means absolute destruction for not only our world, but the order of all worlds in our universe.

In the constellation we know as Beta Persei, there lay Algol; the Demon Star. Mirfak is her Slayer, and Capulus his weapon.

Algol Egregor (worshipers of the Demon Star, in which the Gorgon is just one shade) have been around for eons, long before recorded history. They worship the most primal aspects of the Serpent, and they found that first expression of the Demon Star in the subterranean, chthonic powers of the dark earth. The discarded scales of the serpent are where the properties of Caput Algol burned brightest for them. Not above the earth, but beneath it. Algol Egregor has always been around, but the infernal power of their dark goddess has mainly been kept in check by Mirfak and Capulus. The Demon Star has physically incarnated only twice in our solar system.

Eons ago, on Mars, where she destroyed the planet and nearly (some artifacts remain, as you'll soon learn) every trace of its once mighty civilization. And more recently on our own planet, many ages before the start of mankind's recorded history. She briefly incarnated, but was destroyed by incarnations of Mirfak and Capulus, though not before causing much destruction. The balance was maintained. It's not that way any longer.

The followers of Mirfak and Capulus, along with many of Beta Persei's lesser stars (Mikhab, Atiks, etc..) have all been slaughtered. Their energetic properties have been seized by the leaders of Algol Egregor, through ancient thaumaturgy and abundant human sacrifice.

Mirfak has been engulfed by the wealthy thaumaturge, John Smith, and Capulus, by his second in command. Trevor John, the demon shade. Born of a possessed woman and fathered from the mixed seed of mad men, spat out of the mouth of a rancid whore into Legion's stolen body.

They're now working to incarnate a shade of Algol into a mortal woman, so they can destroy this world and be reborn on the dark scales of their mother.

I can't handle this task, Scorcher. I'm too old and weak. I curse the day I found Ishum while traveling through the Estonian island of Saaremaa. It surfaced at the Kaali crater, a living artifact from our twin planet's dead civilization, originally an ancient gift given to them from Sirius, and the blade Erra, as well. They were both sent to us thousands of years ago by the few remaining inhabitants of Mars, then concealed on the moon Phobos. I was on a trek across Eastern Europe, tracking the underground Neo-Nazi black market, and buying Third Reich artifacts so I could burn them and piss on their ashes. I had heard a rumor that a copy of Heidegger and Himmler's obscure co -written book of poetry named "Pudel, so laß das Heulen! (Himmler had encoded occult scripture into the book without the philosopher's knowledge) was in Estonia, but I only came away with Himmler's personal copy of the old Frisian hoax grimoire, The Oera Linda Book.

It was after pissing on its ashes that I saw the star, and the latch key cloud underneath it. I heard a bark in the dark woods, and followed the specter of my first dog: the long dead Golden Retriever, Little Sandy Koufax.

Ishum was floating on the surface of the dark, water-filled crater.

If I'd only known then that it wasn't a book, but a death sentence! A living thing from beyond our stars, and a gateway between worlds. A cosmic intelligence in its own right, and able to transform its physical structure and our spiritual vision!

When I first found the thing, it was a giant tome, with spells and incantations written by followers of the ancient Goddess Gula, and even older Egyptian writings about Anubis. They're both shades of the Great Star, Sirius. Entire pages would disappear, then reappear in a different order. The content would change from spells to ancient stellar maps, and then journal entries in different languages that I couldn't read but instinctively understood.

Ishum is not a grimoire or journal or clay tablet. It's a weapon and badge of office from Sirius the guardian—the Nile Star.

It changes your vision. It lets you see the world with ancient eyes. It brings you to the Drift, and you either float or crash.

The Great Spirit of that star resurfaced, and chose me to bring Ishum to America where the sword had been buried. And though it's compelled me to write in its pages, I just can't perform the final act of supplication! I won't seal my bloody hand into it and lose the destiny written across my palms! I can't become its vessel! It knows this, and it seeks you. I now believe it always has.

I'm merely the Announcer. The lesser star Murzim, who rises before Sirius, the Scorcher.

I think its protective powers are abandoning me. I've been seeing serpents around the edge of the cemetery: Pythons, diamondbacks, things that should only be at a zoo. There have been less and less stray dogs guarding the gate, and I think one of the homeless guys that camp around here got bitten by a viper. He may be dead in one of those makeshift tents outside the gate.

I can feel Smith and his minions drawing me out. They won't get Ishum, though. I know that much. It has its own methods of self-preservation, it's very shrewd. I doubt they can even physically see the badge of Sirius. They can see the blade, however. It's not alive in the way Ishum is, though it's a much more powerful weapon. Erra can slice through anything. It can destroy the physical, etheric and astral. It demolishes souls, and the shadows of stellar gods. I buried Erra under a large white rock, in front of Jeremiah Clock's gravestone.

It's on the north side of the hill, by the baseball fields. There's a rip in the lower half of the cemetery's chain link fence.

Crawl through it, and unearth the blade, Scorcher.

Things are coming to a head. It's a week before the conjunction. Soon Ishum will leave me.

I just hope it's not you, Jesse Ventura, though I have a feeling it is. Jess, if you found this thing I'm truly sorry. I brought a curse into your life, my friend.

I wish I could have said goodbye before this all went down. I say goodbye now.

Saul Cohen, October 22nd

Jesse placed Ishum down on his bed. He was numb, but everything the dog walker had just read registered in a very deep way. It was a part of him now; it may have even been since childhood. The dog walker thought about his time with Smokey, and he remembered often staring up at the night sky while he was tied up with the Husky. Jesse remembered a strange bright star, and recalled the feeling that it was somehow observing him.

Jesse stood and walked toward his window. He opened it wide, and a chill blast of air rushed through. It was reinvigorating. He looked down at the empty block, at the tenement windows across the street. Most of the shades were drawn. The sky above was a light blue, and he saw a dog-shaped cloud drift across it. It slowly transformed into a latch key, then into the shape of the diary.

"The Shining One. The Scorcher. Sirius of Canis Major," said Jesse as he stared up at it.

Scorcher.

The Dog Walker looked away from the sky. He closed his window. *I have to do something soon*, he thought. The conjunction was tonight. Saul wrote that Algol Egregor had some esoteric way of locating him, drawing him out. Jesse had felt no such pull. The dog walker shook his head, and rubbed the side of his temples. He adjusted the dead mariachi's sombrero and began to pace back and forth nervously in the room.

A shade of the Demon Star, Caput Algol. A Gorgon? Medusa? Jesse suddenly felt manic. He felt like he was going to lose it again, Scorcher or no fucking Scorcher.

Medusa – now that's a fucking hell of a way to get stoned, he thought. *I need to blog about this shit on Fucked in Park Slope. Maybe I can even take a picture of the snake-headed bitch. Post it on Instagram. She probably just wants a reality show on the Oxygen network! Oprah, watch out. Hide Steadman. You have competition. A fucking avatar of a galactic principle that wants to destroy our world because it can't dream the dreams we have while looking up at it! Jesus Christ. No wonder why Saul went crazy and started sleeping in Quaker cemeteries.* Jesse bit his fist. He tried to slow his breathing.

"Alrighty then! I'm no Saul, though. God bless his soul. I'm Jesse Ventura, and I can handle this."

I'm the same Jesse Ventura that stabbed my father in his stomach after he beat my cracked-out mom to a pulp and killed my dog. I grew up in a fucking snake pit, thought Jesse, *and I've seen you coming from miles away. I'm itching to cut your goddamn head off, bitch.*

Jesse calmed down. *The sword, I need that at the very least,* he thought. Every nerve in his body was itching for it now. He looked over at Ishum on the bed. That vaguely recognizable Moleskine diary Jesse had held in his hand only moments before was gone. This thing was now something

142

else completely. Ishum was now a piece of undulating, patina-colored metal. It sparkled wildly.

Now it was just a question of getting to Prospect Park and slipping into the cemetery. It was risky, but this was the only way forward. Dig up Erra, and take it from there. Jesse smiled. He remembered today was Halloween.

He had a fresh change of clothes in his locker, but the costume, well, Marvin Trout kept a wardrobe room in the Den for his LARPing. companions. It was Halloween for them practically every day of the year, after all.

Jesse suddenly became aware of his hunger. He hadn't eaten since yesterday. There was a leftover slice from the takeout he'd ordered two days ago, when the world still made sense. It felt like a lifetime ago. That world was dead to him now. He looked at Ishum. Jesse swallowed hard. Was it, though? Could he erase the destiny written across his palms, forever? He looked down at the small piece of shifting metal. *Only blood can finalize the partnership*, thought Jesse. Ishum responded, as if reading his mind. It transformed into a small book right before his very eyes, opening up to reveal a clean white page.

Jesse turned away. He grinned and swallowed hard. The book closed. Not yet. I'll deal with that when I have to. First thing's first. Jesse took the

143

keys out of his hoodie, and he walked over to his locker. He took out a clean set of clothes and a towel and laid them on his bed. He gently laid the black sombrero on the cot. The dog walker checked his watch. Almost one. He took a shower and was dressed in a black sweatshirt and jeans fifteen minutes later. He quickly gobbled the cold slice of pizza in the Den's kitchen, then he downed a bottle of Evian water. Jesse walked to Marvin's bedroom and quickly backed away. There was a campaign in session.

"Lance me you fucker, deeper!" yelled his elf from Bushwick.

"Yeah! Yeah! Fuck!"

The two LARPers were going at it hard, chaotic evil and lawful neutral alignments notwithstanding. Jesse didn't need to roll seven 20's in a row to realize Bigby's Moan of Climax was nowhere close to being cast. The two had serious stamina points.

"Damn," Jesse mumbled. He stared at the large living room closet. It was where Marvin kept his costumes.

"Fuck me like an ogre!"

"I'd bet you'd like that! Yeah!"

Jesse sneered and stepped away from the door.

"What the fuck is wrong with these people? Weirdos."

It sounded like a bureau got knocked down, glass shattered. The couple kept pounding and moaning, shouting at one another lustfully in Eldarin. Jesse walked over to Marvin's closet and tested the knob. It opened.

"Oh, shit. Yes!" whispered Jesse as he looked over his shoulder. The couple's melee continued, louder and more impassioned than before. He looked inside the brightly lit closet. It stretched back nearly ten feet, and there were costume racks on both sides: cleric robes and chain mail, fantastical masks and weapon props.

"Fuck it. I'll deal with him later. If I live." Jesse stepped inside. He quickly rifled through the wardrobe. He grabbed a heavy black robe and a red orc mask, small rubber tusks jutted out from its jaw. Jesse listened. Amy and Marvin were still going at it. Curiosity got the best of the dog walker, and he examined the prop crate. There was something that didn't look all that fantastical sticking out of it. Jesse touched the gun's cold handle. He lifted the wooden lid, then shook his head in disbelief. Two Uzis, a sawed-off shotgun, and numerous semiautomatic pistols were jammed inside the box.

"Holy shit. This fucking guy."

Jesse suddenly smelled weed. He opened another container next to the gun crate and found pounds of hydro and crystal meth. Jesse looked at the weapons again. Fuck it. Jesse grabbed a 22-caliber pistol, and a clip. He secured it along his waistband and quickly placed everything back in its rightful place.

Jesse crept out of the closet, and shut the door carefully. He dashed back into his room. He put on his costume, then picked up the thing disguised as a book and placed it inside the black robe's inside pocket. Ishum felt right next to his chest, and it radiated a fresh surge of warmth and vigor. Jesse left his room, and moments later, the apartment. The campaign in Marvin's room continued, with no   end   in   sight.

XII
BETTER THAN ACID

Jesse stepped out onto the chilly street. He was the only orc on the block. He rushed north, and covered three avenues in five minutes. Adults gawked at him on Fifth, and children pointed and laughed.

Shit. Maybe this isn't such a good idea, thought Jesse. *I'm drawing too much attention to myself.*

Still, he understood that his disguise would be a necessity in Park Slope. It was also likely that there would be a lot more adults in costume in that neighborhood. He would blend in easier. If Jesse hadn't lost his cash and his wallet he would have just taken the train. He now had no choice but to troop it. He walked onto Fifty-Fifth Street, heading toward Sixth Avenue. It was a quieter and less populated route.

The block had tidy apartment buildings and small houses on both sides of the street. A short, blonde-haired man with a horse-face was yanked out of a beige house by his hyperactive beagle. They were across the street from Jesse. The dog snapped its head around to stare at him.

"Sit," he whispered, knowing the beagle would somehow hear.

The dog instantly sat down, nearly tripping his perplexed walker. Jesse stopped to watch. He then closed his eyes, and visualized the dog making a mad dash toward the next building. He heard the man yell in surprise. Jesse opened his eyes. He watched the beagle pull up in front of the apartment building, owner barely holding onto its leash.

"What's gotten into you, Tatonka?"

"Good dog," said Jesse quietly. He turned away and headed up the street. Ishum was just giving him a taste of its abilities. Jesse could feel a massive power surge in the transformed book. It was changing him, as well. Jesse walked along the quiet stretch of Sixth Avenue from Fifty-Fifth Street on down, feeling an overwhelming sense of power. He had some type of preternatural connection with canines now, more potent than ever before. Jesse could feel them watching him from behind closed windows, could hear their distant howling. The dog walker felt a fire blazing in his veins. This was a fierce gift from his star, Sirius.

A man smoking a Newport walked past him on Forty-Fifth Street, and Jesse concentrated on the cigarette's small, glowing ember. The dog walker focused and intensified it with thought, and when Jesse saw the tip of the Newport burst into flame he realized he may not even need Marvin's gun.

The man screamed and tossed the cigarette onto the sidewalk as the dog walker strode by. Jesse hurried past Fortieth Street. Even though he was an avenue away from his apartment, he figured they still might be circling the block. He saw nothing suspicious, however.

The dog walker was by Greenwood Cemetery within fifteen minutes. He walked along the empty sidewalk, and looked beyond the black gate at its green rolling fields. He thought about the dead hidden inside of them. Jesse had never truly considered death, or anything deeply metaphysical up until now. The dog walker went still. He peered into the graveyard. He had never been inside a cemetery. His dead mother had been cremated by an aunt he never spoke to, and his father was rotting in some Potter's Field.

Jesse watched a Milky Way wrapper blow across a series of plots. Ishum beat hard across his chest. He listened to the cemetery's silence. Saul said there was life after death. It was a special gift we had, or rather one our solar system was imbued with. Death was a gateway out of our strand of the Multiverse. Whatever that meant.

The graveyard held only silence for the dog walker. He didn't feel anything. A strong wind blew the Milky Way wrapper toward his foot, and he thoughtlessly kicked it away. Jesse walked on, much closer to Park Slope now. He was nearing the cemetery's southern edge.

Jesse approached a young South Slope couple with a small child dressed like a turtle. The man and woman were both dressed like the Thin White Duke, and they smiled at Jesse. The toddler giggled and kicked out of its baby carriage, exhilarated by the sight of the monster in which Jesse was hidden. His mind raced. Can I tell who's who? Will I just know Algol Egregor when I see them? Will the diary alarm me?

The dog walker's gut told him he would recognize them when he saw them. Jesse had already started to *see* things since he started this trek twenty blocks back.

The world around him was shifting and becoming thinner. Jesse could see traces of alien starshine in the shadows along the avenue. He could feel the strange heat of Sirius coating the chill autumn wind as it rustled through trees and whispered strange ambrosial melodies into his ear.

Jesse didn't need to look up at the sky to know he was being watched. He could feel clouds tracking him overhead, prompted by stalking constellations. This was like no high Jesse had ever experienced before, and he had dropped a fair amount of acid in his twenty-nine years. This was better   than   acid. No, this was a different state entirely. Saul was right. This was floating. Drifting. And it felt natural, like an ancient faculty that had been lost over time. Jesse felt that in his core— as above, so below.

Jesse was euphoric. His body didn't ache; it didn't even feel like he had a body. Was this what Saul was really afraid of? This feeling of walking on air? Of being air?

I could get use to this. Get ready Medusa, the Scorcher is coming, the dog walker thought as he glided along the pavement.

XIII
PARK SLOPE

Jesse drifted into Park Slope. He had unconsciously wandered back onto Fifth Avenue, and a bit of the euphoria left him as trendy coffee shops and ill-fitting condos lurched over old bodegas and 99-cent stores. Jesse saw two South Slope stroller moms pushing their carriages along the street halfway up Twentieth and Fifth. They were dressed like haloed angels, but Jesse saw something else. Serpent-formed shadows were gathered around the two, and they danced hypnotically along the sidewalk.

Jesse had to pull himself back. For an instant, despite everything, he had actually felt like walking over to them. This is what Saul meant: their drawing him in. As they approached, Jesse realized that the mothers may not even be consciously using those strange shadows to compel him. It was this psychedelic state. Drifting encouraged it. It loosened something vital in you, something essential. You were open.

The two angels walked past him, and they became silent. They could sense something, as they glared at him in his black robe and orc mask.

The women slowed their pace. They seemed to be scrutinizing Jesse's shadow as it trailed along his side. The dog walker had been able to sneak into the Diamondback, but he wasn't carrying Ishum at the time. Things were different now.

Ishum beat hard against his chest. Their shadows tried to test his own. They began to stretch wide and encircle it. Jesse stopped walking. He shifted the diary away from his chest, and he willed himself out of the Drift. Jesse felt a sudden heavy shift, his pockets felt lined with stones. The serpent shadows faded as he stepped toward the women with his right hand out.

"You ladies got a dollar? I need to— "

They looked at one another and sneered, then quickly pushed their strollers up the street. The dog walker smiled. He knew that move would send them on their way. Jesse stood in front of a newly built yoga studio, and it felt like he had suddenly been weighed down with two hundred additional pounds. The dog walker was breathing heavily, physical pain was returning.

He had stopped Drifting by moving Ishum away from his chest, but more importantly by not wanting to Drift, no matter how good it felt. The dog walker realized he now had some control over it. Still, control wasn't mastery. That would come when he spilled blood into the Ishum, sealing the pact.

Jesse quickly put the diary in his outer pocket as he walked forward. He picked up his pace. He was a good ten blocks away from Prospect Park. He should have stayed on Sixth Avenue. This area was too populated. Bar hoppers were already out, and they stumbled past small families trick-or-treating at Trader Joes and Whole Foods. Jesse was right, though. There were a lot more adults in costume. He didn't stand out. He walked past the drunken crew members of *Star Trek: The Next Generation*. A fat Data drunkenly stumbled around the street and nearly collided into Jesse.

"Fuck you, Shrek! You think you own the sidewalk!" he screamed. Fat drunk Data fell onto the ground, giggled, and clawed up at the air. His crew didn't help him.

Jesse said nothing. He walked quickly onto the next block. The dog walker could still feel eyes on his back, even though he wasn't Drifting. He walked past yet another coffee shop, and Jesse saw a blonde woman with a sour face watching him with hostility in her eyes through the window as she breast fed her baby.

He jogged off Fifth and up toward the next avenue. A quiet, tree-lined block with condos wedged uncomfortably in between small two-story houses. Somebody cursed at him from a moving car. Jesse ignored it. The dog walker was paranoid, and his body ached, but he kept the influence of Ishum at bay. And he kept moving.

Jesse strode onto Seventh Avenue. There were tons of people out. It almost looked like a block in Midtown Manhattan during rush hour.

"What the hell, man. Everyone decide to take a personal   day?" More families trick-or-treating and grown men dressed like Alex from *A Clockwork Orange* skateboarded past him. Drunken revelers and tweens with yoga mats floated past cafe after cafe, bar after bar.

He suspected that they could all see through his disguise. Jesse couldn't see through theirs, and relying on Ishum would make him even easier to spot. He was now completely sure of that. The dog walker's steps became uncertain. Jesse began to shudder and hyperventilate whenever he saw a mother with a baby stroller.

Jesse started sidestepping them on rubbery legs, always managing to crane his neck and look inside of the pushcart before doing so. He hardly ever saw a baby, just bundles of clothes and blankets that might have been covering up a dead cat or raccoon. He shook his orcish head, then touched the gun on his waist. Jesse was disoriented. He had walked four blocks to 10th Street without even realizing it. The dog walker doubled back toward 14th Street.

Nightmare scenes from the Diamondback flashed across his mind. Billy Ocean's "Caribbean Queen" began to play repeatedly in his head. Jesse needed Ishum next to his chest again. He was losing his nerve. The world was crashing down around him.

Waves of people passed by. Loud voices talking about gluten-free diets and heart chakras, spiced pumpkin beer and Roman Polanski movie nights. He needed to get off the sidewalk for a minute. Jesse heard a bark, then another, and another. He turned and looked at the window of a pet shelter. Two German Shepherds and several mutts were staring at him, and barking wildly. People were beginning to glare at Jesse. He needed to get away. Jesse sprinted up the street, and he ran inside the first shop he saw.

Lil Puffin's Big Ole House O Muffin.

The shop was small and warm. Pictures of puffins and muffins lined its bright orange walls.

"Hi. Welcome to Lil Puffin's Big Ole House O Muffin. How may I help you?" asked a sexually androgynous   voice. Jesse stared into the face of the transgender muffin shop barista. She looked a bit like Terry Richardson and Amy Adams. The dog walker then stared around the muffin shop nervously. He saw that it was empty, for the most part. The only other patron was an Ecuadorian guy with an eerie resemblance to John Mayer. He was innocently strumming a small banjo in the corner. Jesse looked at the transwoman's name tag. Wanda stared at Jesse impatiently.

"Can I help you?"

"Give me a second," Jesse said, while catching his breath. He walked over to a table and sat down. Wanda stared at him angrily. The banjo player was oblivious to everything but his instrument.

The world was settling back down a bit, though he knew the enemy was onto him. He stood up and looked out the window. He saw a red-haired stroller mom standing across the street.

The red-headed stroller mom. She had watched Jesse from the park bench, and been a part of Smith's bizarre desecration of Ginger's corpse. She was standing in place and wheeling a massive baby carriage back and forth along the sidewalk. The woman gazed at Jesse, an American Spirit cigarette dangling from the side of her mouth.

"Mr. Shrek! Are you going to order something or just be random and creepy?"

Jesse faced Wanda. "Trick-or-treat."

"Excuse you?"

"What do you have for fifty-cents?

The barista stared at him contemptuously. "I don't know, dumbass. Maybe fifty fucking crumbs?"

Jesse looked back out the window. The stroller mom was now on her cell phone.

He had to make a move. Jesse saw a fat dachshund passing by with a blonde-haired female dog walker. They were ambling behind the cult member. Jesse held on tight to Ishum. He closed his eyes and felt instantly weightless, buoyant.

He focused, and visualized the dog biting the menacing pram pusher. Jesse heard a scream.

"My God!" hollered Wanda as she ran to the window.

Jesse bolted out onto the sidewalk. The woman's screams of pain were deafening. Jesse ran to the corner of Fourteenth Street, and he didn't stop running until he was nearly an avenue away. He leaned up against a small elm tree, breathing heavily. He lifted his mask for a moment and sucked in the cold air. Jesse was close to Eighth Avenue. He heard a commotion from behind. He put the mask back on, then looked over his shoulder. He faced a Park Slope mob. Two biracial stroller moms pushed heavy Maclaren metal alongside two lumberjack-bearded white men in flannel jackets and skinny jeans. A heavy-set Asian woman wearing a beige fedora and denim overalls strode in front of a skinny gay couple holding hands. The Latino man was dressed like Fred Flintstone, his black boyfriend, Wilma. All of their attention was focused on Jesse. And they all wore horn-rimmed glasses.

Jesse began to power walk up the rest of the street. He glanced back, and saw them moving quickly. He knew they would start to run after him any moment now. *Would they really try to grab me in broad daylight?* thought Jesse. The conjunction was near, and he could sense their desperation. They were capable of anything.

"Murderer!" yelled the Latino Fred Flintstone.

Jesse grabbed the butt of his pistol. He had never held a gun before today, much less shot anything. Jesse realized that he hadn't even loaded the   clip.
He rushed toward the edge of the street. A helmeted rider on a red Vespa suddenly burst onto the avenue in front of Jesse. The dog walker looked over his shoulder. The mob was dangerously close. The Vespa driver eyed him.

I need a miracle, thought Jesse.

He looked across the avenue, and his prayers were instantly answered. Three miracles, actually, and they stood in front of a deli, along with one annoying hex.

Victor was posted up on the corner of Eighth Avenue and 14th Street, eating from a bag of Kale chips. He had three massive pit bulls with him. He was standing in front of the deli, catcalling any woman unfortunate enough to walk by. Victor was dressed up like Indiana Jones. He had a small jump rope on his waist instead of a whip.

Jesse bolted past the Vespa rider and across the street.

"Heel," he whispered to the three pit bulls, not wanting to alarm them. They all dropped to their haunches at once, almost pulling Victor down with them. He had never seen these dogs before, yet they obeyed.

"What the fuck, guys?" griped Victor.

Jesse ran up to them. The three pit bulls wagged their tails. Victor jumped back, staring in alarm at the orc-faced dog walker.

"Yo, who you...?"

"It's Jesse Ventura."

Victor suddenly laughed. He shook his head up and down as he stared at Jesse. His cornrows spilled out from underneath his brown fedora.

"Ahh... I recognize that fake Puerto Rican yuppie voice anywhere, bro. You didn't even have to say your name. Why you dressed like a Shrek, Jesse Ventura, the pussy version?"

"I'm in trouble. I need to cut a deal with you."

Jesse faced the crowd across the street. They were assembling on the corner, and watching him intently.

Jesse closed his eyes. He imagined the dogs going ballistic and ripping out of Victor's grip, running to the edge of the curb and stopping there as they barked monstrously.

"Hey, what the hell, guys?"

They barked and growled at the Park Slope mob. Jesse opened his eyes and smiled.

They got the message, and some began to filter back up the block. The others walked into a small cafe, where they continued to watch Jesse. The Vespa rider zoomed off. The dogs continued to bark.

"Heel!" Victor screamed. His bag of kale chips were crushed underfoot.

"Heel," Jesse whispered, and the dogs stopped barking all at once.

The pit bulls ran up to Jesse, eager to be petted.

"This happens whenever you're around. How you do that shit?"

"I need to cut a deal with you, Victor. I need your help," Jesse said heavily.

All Jesse actually needed was the protection of the dogs; he didn't even really need Victor. He could Drift and compel the dogs to follow, but that would mean drawing Algol Egregor once more. They already had a beat on him, but he could change out of costume in the park. Jesse needed to convince Victor to come with him to Prospect. He couldn't continue to use Ishum's power anymore, at this point.

"You make a deal with *me?* You creepy, satanic motherfucka. Who are you to make a deal with me?"

Jesse took off his mask. Victor stared at him in shock.

"Damn, kid! You got fucked up!"

"People are trying to kill me."

Victor stared him up and down. The three pit bulls stood their ground patiently.

"Really? Why's that? And don't tell me it's because of dog walking."

"Yeah. It's because of dog walking."

Jesse puts his mask back on. He looked over his shoulder on the other side of the avenue. A stroller mom watched him from around the corner, poking her head out. Victor followed Jesse's gaze. He whistled and waved at the woman. "Eh yo mami! Ah ha! Come over here, Becky! Karen? You need a dog walker? A babysitter? A midday lover? I do it all!"

The woman looked away in disgust. She disappeared around the corner.

"Was that one of your wannabe murderers?"

"Walk me to the park, Victor. I'll explain everything."

"Do it here, bro."

"Just level with me, man. I'm not safe. People want to kill me. I'm talking about giving you all my contacts. All my clients."

Silence. Victor nodded.

"Ok. I'll walk with you. But make it quick."

Jesse spoke frantically as they powerwalked up the street. By the time they were next to Prospect Park Jesse was the one leading the three dogs.

"That's the stupidest shit I ever heard, bro! The Russian mob is out to get you because you rescued a fighting dog?"

"Keep your voice down."

The three pit bulls snapped at Victor.

"Slow your roll, man," Victor said, shuffling back toward the curb.

"It's all good. Come on."

They edged across the entrance of the park, walking through the Fourteenth Street section. A playground and bandshell were on their left-hand side, stretches of green field on their right. The path to the cemetery was a straight walk, across the road and baseball diamonds and up a hill.

Jesse looked at the playground, and saw that it was empty except for a West Indian nanny and a small bundled up white child playing on a swing set. There were a few teenagers wandering around the bandshell, cutting school. They were dressed all in black, and some wore plastic *Scream* masks. This section of the park was empty for the most part. Jesse breathed a sigh of relief as he led the three massive pit bulls toward the road. Victor trailed behind.

"Why would you give up dog walking, man? You're like a dog whisperer. Look at the way you got Menace, Killer and Hazard actin'. I've been walking them for years. You only known them ten minutes and you got control."

Jesse stared at the road. A few joggers and a Parks Department van moved lazily behind them. Jesse had slowly stopped Drifting. The clouds and shadows were normal, and he couldn't hear strange stellar melodies playing along the rustle of leaves and snapping branches anymore. His keen telepathic control of the canines was dramatically lessened, as well. This would hopefully stop Algol Egregor from honing in, for the moment at least. Jesse looked back at Victor.

"You weren't listening, Victor. I never said I was giving up the 'game.' I said I was leaving New York. You can have all my connects, man. I'm moving to California. More money out there."

"The celebrity dog walking game," said Victor ponderously.

"You betcha!" blurted Jesse, only half hearing his rival. He was growing impatient.

"Maybe your own reality television show."

"Yeah. Maybe."

Silence. Jesse looked over his shoulder. The nanny in the playground and the teenagers cutting school paid them no mind. The coast remained clear, though certainly not for long. The dog walkers were about fifteen yards away from the road, and slowly walking up the hill by some picnic tables.

"But I don't understand. Why me?" Jesse stopped. The three pit bulls leaped onto him playfully. He almost fell.

"Heel," he said, and they obediently sat down at once. Jesse turned to face Victor, and he stared at him with a dour expression. He said the next sentence with a straight face.

"You've been my greatest enemy, and because of that, you've been my greatest ally."

Victor shrugged. "Really?"

"Yes. Really."

"The word is frenemy. I'm your greatest frenemy"

"Sure."

Victor gave Jesse a wide smile.

"How many words I got to teach you? I been tryin' to teach you to speak better Spanish all these years. You know I always looked at you like a little half- white brother. One I gotta fuck with so he—"

"Yeah, yeah. Ok. I get the point."

Jesse picked up a large branch. He flung it, and let go of their leashes. The three pit bulls ran after it. Killer and Menace clamped down on opposite sides of the stick, and they tugged violently. Hazard tried to muscle in.

"I'll introduce you to my clients over the next few days. Make it official. So what's up? We got a deal?"

"Sure, it sounds good, bro. I still don't believe you all the way, you know, but I'll have to wait and see."

"But you're down?" Jesse asked, looking over his shoulder at the park's entrance. He still didn't see anybody. Jesse whistled, calling the three pit bulls over. They dropped the branch and ran to him at once.

"Yeah."

"I need a favor right now though, man. I need you to keep watch for me while I get something from that hill."

Jesse turned and pointed across the road, toward the wooded hill. "But— "

"I know. What's in it for you *today,* right?"

Victor smiled and nodded.

"Yep."

"I'll give you a client later. I'll cancel, say you're my replacement. That's $500 cash," Jesse said, and he wasn't lying. He actually did have an appointment later on in the day.

They were still standing by the picnic tables on the hill. Jesse was ready to get going. "I gotta bring the dogs back soon," Victor said.

"How soon?"

"Before five."

"I'll be done in less than fifteen minutes."

"Ok. Fuck it. Whatever, bro."

Jesse gave Victor his dogs back.

"Go first. I'll meet you up there in a minute. I got to change."

Jesse turned quickly, and he ran behind a tree. Victor shook his head. He cursed under his breath, then walked across the road. Jesse watched him go, then he quickly took off his mask and cloak. Jesse left the costume by the tree, and headed toward   the   cemetery.

XIV
THE QUAKER CEMETERY

They stopped on a small dirt road on top of the hill. The dog walkers were hidden by a long line of oak trees still clinging stubbornly to the rags of their summer garment, now a mottled gold and burgundy. The Quaker cemetery was only a few yards behind and above Jesse's shoulder, hidden inside the wood line.

Victor held onto the leashes of his three pit bulls tightly. They were seated patiently.

"If you see anybody, whistle. If a stranger gets too curious, then just intimidate them with the dogs and make them go away."

Victor stared at him blankly.

"Just fucking make it quick, dude."

"I will. I just have to grab the ring my old girlfriend tossed over the gate. I know where it's at, so don't worry. "

Victor stared at him incredulously. "Uh, yeah. That's probably a lie. But whatever. Let's just speed it up." Victor turned away from Jesse. He looked up and down the jogging trail. The dog walker took out the .22 and jammed the clip in. He handed the pistol to Victor.

"What the fuck?!? You a G, now?"

"For protection."

"What the hell did I get myself into?" Victor asked, taking the pistol and concealing it in his brown leather jacket.

"I love you Indy," Jesse whispered, imitating Short Round from *The Temple of Doom*.

"Fuckin' go already, man!"

Jesse turned and hurried past the wood line, further up the hill. He saw the chain link fence and suddenly remembered the Diamondback as he pushed through the bushes. He slowed his pace, eyes on the ground. He reached the gate. About twenty yards off to his right were two small tents and what looked to be the remnants of a campfire in between them. Vagrants.

Or Algol Egregor, thought Jesse nervously. The dog walker shrugged. The area looked empty now, for what it was worth. He looked at the gate again.

"Thank God," he said, almost instantly finding the tear in the chain link. Saul's entrance was a gash at the very bottom of the gate. It was about four feet wide and clearly made with a bolt cutter. Jesse would have to crawl.

The dog walker peered into the cemetery. It was overrun with weeds, and most of the tombstones were moss and lichen covered, ancient looking. Saul said the blade was buried by a tombstone with the name Jeremiah Clock on it, a former Harbinger of Sirius. It was somewhere around this section of the cemetery.

Jesse got on his knees and he laid out flat. He crawled on his stomach through the rip in the gate. He heard a loud groan and crash from the campsite area.

Jesse bolted up quickly and looked over his shoulder at the tents. Nothing. He wiped dead leaves and dirt off his body. The sharp wind sliced at him and he shivered. Jesse looked around and didn't see cameras or people anywhere. Security had to be lax. Saul was basically living here. The cemetery looked ancient and out of place. Strange that it was located in one of Brooklyn's most commercial neighborhoods.

He looked up the cemetery's sloping hill and saw nothing but trees, bushes and more gravestones. Jesse started inspecting the markers. Most didn't even have names or dates, but the ones that did went all the way back to the 1700s.

Jesse heard a loud noise off to his left. He turned and saw a giant raccoon stumble past a tombstone. It stopped and stared at him for a moment, then it hustled to the gate. The animal jumped on top of the chain link fence and climbed over. It plopped down on the dirt and scrambled toward the bushes. The raccoon suddenly barked in alarm, then it dropped instantly out of sight, down into the shrub.

"What the fuck?" Jesse continued to watch the tents on other side of the gate for several moments, but he saw and heard nothing, so he walked on.

A strong breeze shuffled dead leaves at his feet. He began to notice remnants of Saul's strange graveyard tenure: empty packs of cigarettes, fast food containers, a few Jamba Juice cups, and a large, leather duffel bag. Jesse picked it up, then looked inside.

A set of keys, and the address to Saul's cabin in the Missouri Ozarks written on a crumpled piece of paper, a roll of hundred-dollar bills and Saul's credit cards. The dog walker put everything back in the bag and placed it on the ground.

Saul had written that Algol Egregor couldn't physically step into this place. They could barely register it. That meant Saul had truly given up and left this safe zone, no longer able to fight the compulsion to join Algol Egregor. Jesse's heart sank. He pushed the image of Saul's decapitated head out of his mind and trudged forward.

He heard another loud rustling noise over his shoulder. He turned and saw nothing. Jesse kept moving. He put his head down and observed the markers. The dog walker saw two Jebediahs in succession, but no Jeremiah – a Constance and a Maben. He walked further up. Ishum was starting to grow warm. It was letting Jesse know in which direction to walk.

"Hot and cold, I see."

The game didn't last long. He walked another two meters, and the book nearly scorched his waist.

"The Scorcher," he said, standing over the graveyard of the harbinger.

A raven cawed and circled overhead, as it flew darkly against the now cloudless sky. Silence besides that. Jesse looked over his shoulder once again at the tents. They were gone. The dog walker cursed under his breath.

He shook his head and wondered if Victor was still even down there. He had to put that out of his mind for now. Jesse looked back down at the grave. A large white stone was at its foot. Jesse moved it with his sneaker, revealing a hidden world of wet soil and insects.

He got on his knees and began to dig with his bare hands.

The insect-covered dirt flew over his shoulders, earthworms and centipedes went airborne. Jesse dug frantically. Frost streamed out of his mouth, and he wondered how far below the sword was buried, if it was there at all. Jesse worked furiously, like a man possessed. He gritted his teeth and tunneled deep, panting heavily. After a few minutes, his fingers touched cold metal.

Jesse snatched the long iron box from the earth. Its lock was snapped open. The dog walker nearly gasped when he saw what was inside.

Jesse reverently took Erra out of its burgundy scabbard. It sparkled intensely under the autumn sun, far surpassing its glare. An engraving of the star Sirius was etched in gold along the cyan-shaded metal. There were glistening rubies and pieces of dark green moldavite inlaid on the hilt of the blade. Erra was the size of a short sword, and it looked sharper than a katana. The burgundy colored scabbard, however, was plain. There was a gold chain strapped to it.

Jesse stood, hacking and slashing at thin air. Erra felt alive in his hand. The same electric feeling Jesse had when he first laid eyes on the badge of Sirius coursed through him. Ishum nearly jumped out of his pocket. Jesse knew what he had to do. All doubt was gone. He sliced his palm with the blade. The blood started to flow. Jesse put Erra down and quickly took out Ishum. The diary had transformed into a humanoid hand.

Jesse clenched it with his own bloody hand. He felt an electrical surge, and Ishum squeezed back. There was no pain when a thin stream of blue fire shot up from his palm and quickly spread all over his body, engulfing him for several moments, and then it stopped as abruptly as it started. Jesse stood there, clothes and skin completely unburnt.

The badge of Sirius had crawled up his left forearm. It was now a cinnabar colored gauntlet, and it felt like hardened steel. Jesse looked around, and saw that he was Drifting. Everything looked psychedelic once again.

The Drift was much more vivid and intense now. Jesse tried to leave that state, but he couldn't. This was it. He realized he could control and minimize it, by imagining the color and vitality of the world evaporating into a pinprick of darkness. All vision disappeared.

He was in total darkness.

"No..." he whispered.

Jesse was blind.

He would never see the world the same way again. Jesse had absolutely no sight when he wasn't Drifting. This was the deal, total immersion, an absolute engagement. No longer watching the shadows on Plato's cave wall; but either seeing them in technicolor, or suffering a complete darkness.

Jesse tried to hold back tears. There was no way to avoid detection from Algol Egregor without going into total darkness. Jesse let the light return, and it did. There was too much of it. It was like being on unholy amounts of peyote. The sensory overload was making him hyperventilate. Jesse wiped the tears from his eyes.

He picked up Erra. It was radiating an azure light.

Jesse suddenly heard Victor's whistle, loud and nervous.   Once.   Twice. The Scorcher then heard something else: a quick rustle of leaves, the sorrowful moan of the wind. Jesse smelled death. Then he turned and saw it, standing by the gate, smiling at him.

It was a dead homeless man, yet it wasn't. Victor whistled again.

"I knew it was you. I always knew it was you," said   the   corpse   in   Trevor   John's   voice.

XV
VICTOR LOOKS OUT

The two joggers had burst onto the dirt path in silence. They were dressed identically, black tracksuits and red Pumas. The young, light-skinned black woman was grinning madly. Her jet-black eyes were wet with a liquid too red to be tears.

Trevor John was her running mate.

Victor stepped back. He'd been standing in silence for over ten minutes. It was a personal record. He didn't hear their approach. They seemed to materialize out of thin air.

He tried to whistle, but he couldn't. The three pit bulls stood. They stared at the strange joggers, alarmed.

The duo gazed at Victor. His ears popped. Victor whistled, but the sound was weak, faded. He nervously moved up the hill, dragging the three dogs along. There was now more than enough space for the joggers to pass.

Menace, Killer and Hazard growled at the duo. The noise was muffled, however. Their growls sounded eerie and distant.

"Sorry. Didn't mean to block your way," said Victor, voice frail and ephemeral.

They continued to run in place.

"What the fuck, bro?"

Victor whistled weakly again, and he looked up the hill. The two joggers followed his gaze. Victor sucked his teeth.

"Are you going to fucking pass through or what?"

They instantly stopped jogging. Victor squinted at them. He noticed something strange. Neither jogger had a shadow.

"He's up there, isn't he?" growled Trevor John.

"Who?"

The three pit bulls tried to bark but couldn't.

"The dog walker. You're looking out for him. We know this."

"I don't know what the fuck you talking about, you ugly ass Willy Wonka. Keep it moving. Your creepy-ass face is hurting my eyes."

Victor touched the butt of his pistol. Trevor John took another step forward. The woman continued to grin at Victor. Her features seemed to distort right before his eyes. Her face was distending, then unevenly settling back into place. Thin streaks of blood flowed from her eyes. Victor blinked hard. He looked away from her.

"Scorcher, I know he's near," the man-thing whispered.

Victor loosened his hold on the pit bulls. They stepped boldly toward Trevor John.

"Fuck off, you big ugly motherfucker. I'll slap that pompadour off your fuckin' head."

Trevor John smiled at Victor, his teeth blindingly white.

"What the fuck?" Victor said, staring at the thing's open mouth.

"I've found a body," said Trevor John suddenly.

He collapsed to the ground, going instantly unconscious. The normal sounds of the park returned, no longer distorted. The woman stepped forward. Something hidden beneath her skin began to stretch the surface of her face outward by at least a foot for several heartbeats, then it abruptly snapped back with a meaty thud. Victor watched on in horror as two swirls of darkness appeared behind her, twin serpent shadows. They rushed straight toward Victor. He whistled once. Then twice. He let go of the dogs. Victor grabbed the gun, and he pointed it at her. He whistled again. The pit bulls dodged the shadows. Victor didn't.

They passed through him, and he froze. The dog walker tried to move forward, but he was paralyzed. He dropped the gun, tried to scream, but he could barely move his tongue. Victor couldn't blink. Tears streamed down his face. The serpent shadows raced back behind the woman. The pit bulls were frozen in fear, and they whimpered along the edges of the jogging path.

The woman took her clothes off. She was covered in scars and burn marks. She grinned lewdly at Victor, streams of blood flowing from her obsidian eyes. Blood was flowing in torrents from other parts of her body. Victor watched in horror as she stuck her hand between her legs. She cupped her blood, and then began to toss it onto her twin serpent shadows. She laughed. They fed. Victor watched, unable to move or scream.

XVI
HEARING THE DEAD

Jesse gripped Erra. The unnatural heat of the blade spread from his fingertips to the rest of his body. The dead vagrant stepped forward. His teeth were black and rotten.

"I knew it was you. Gonna kill you like we killed your friend, gonna skull fuck you like I skull fucked him."

Jesse saw Trevor John's demonic shadow projecting from the vagrant's body, horned and insectile. The dog walker's new eyes saw a cloud of dark, gnat- like creatures extending out from the circumference of the possessed man. They bit into the bright, psychedelic landscape of the Quaker cemetery.

"Strong now. She will soon appear. We found this place, and are strong enough to ride carrion and enter."

The Scorcher stepped forward. He readied Erra. The corpse smiled, then stepped back.

"Your human sight is gone, and now you truly see. You can't hide from it. How does it feel? Now you see why this world must end. Can you see the rot? Can you hear them yet? The dead. Listen."

Jesse took another step toward the monster. A beam of light flashed off the blade toward the corpse. He dodged it. "Listen!"

The Scorcher suddenly heard disembodied voices all around him, screaming in anguish.

"There is no heaven anymore, dog walker. It has abandoned this world. Souls burn in hell, or they languish in purgatory. They don't go to heaven. They don't reincarnate. And they don't pass beyond oblivion to other stellar realms. The human spirit has grown incapable of that feat. That gift is wasted on this species, and on this solar system! We will take the gift to our dark mother! Would you like to hear your pare— "

Jesse ran at him, swinging the blade wildly. The corpse dropped to the dirt, lifeless. Erra struck nothing. Trevor John's shadow leaped onto the gate like a mantis. The circle of shifting darkness bit at Jesse, but the heat from the blade quickly dispelled it. Jesse looked down at the corpse. It was now mummified, a husk. Completely drained. The voices of the dead continued to scream all around him.

"Would you like to hear Mommy and Daddy? They've been asking about you," taunted Trevor John's demonic shadow from atop the gate.

"Jesse, you little piece of shit!" His father's voice was in his left ear. Jesse screamed, then pointed Erra at Trevor John's shadow. It flew backwards, out of the cemetery and down the hill.

The dead grew silent once again. Jesse could no longer feel his dead father's hot breath in his ear. Ishum was vibrating. It now nearly covered his entire left arm, from wrist to shoulder. Jesse walked back toward the white stone. He picked up Erra's scabbard and Saul's duffel bag. He placed the scabbard inside of it, then he slung it over his shoulder. He sidestepped the corpse then ran to the gate. The Scorcher sliced through it. He ran down the hill, and suddenly froze. A giant green boa was eating a raccoon. Only the raccoon's head remained, and it projected from the snake's open mouth. It stared at Jesse with a blank expression. The dog walker noticed other shapes slithering along the hill. Jesse swallowed hard. He stepped forward, raising his blade.

Trevor John's catatonic body suddenly bolted upright, as the naked woman stepped past it. The pit bulls growled at her, but scurried off to the side. She stopped and turned to face Trevor John, wiping the blood from her eyes. The monster stared around dizzily. Trevor John looked as if he had just gotten off a rickety roller coaster. He appeared to be dazed and nauseous.

Victor watched in frozen terror. The serpent shadows still danced behind the woman and lashed out threateningly at the pit bulls.

"Did you— "

"No," Trevor John said irritably. "But he's up there, and he has the blade. I'm drained. I can't." He shook his head miserably, spat on the ground, then glared at Victor. There was a look of pure malice on Trevor John's twisted face. He walked forward, pushing the scarred woman out of his way. The pit bulls bared their teeth and barked some more, but did nothing. The serpent shadows snapped at the dogs, keeping them at bay. Trevor John looked down at the gun on the ground. He picked it up, and grinned at Victor.

"Did you think this could stop us?"

Victor's ears popped again, and everything went quiet. Trevor John put the gun under his own arm pit. He pulled the trigger and shot himself, spending the entire round. Victor looked on in disbelief as Trevor John smiled, bullets flying out of his shoulder. Burning blood splattered Victor's face. Trevor John suddenly threw the gun in the direction of the pit bull. It hit Menace in the head. The dog jumped back. The strange veil of silence was lifted. Victor stared at Trevor John. The monster was smiling. His left arm hung off its socket.

"My mother was Legion in the flesh, and I was born from the collective seed of madman gathered and spat out of the mouth of a rancid whore. I was born in less than 90 hours, and I have lived more than 90,000 days. I've stripped and corrupted the power of a fixed star, and I now hold its power. I am Capulus, and I will not decapitate my goddess. I will instead cut her bonds, and she will ravage this world. A feeble guardian of the star Sirius can't stop me, but you suppose a gun could?"

Trevor John spit into his own hand. He rubbed it on his shoulder, and he pressed in. The arm was seamlessly reconnected. Trevor John smiled.

"Voila!" he screamed. His blonde pompadour shook.

Trevor John stepped in front of Victor.

"You know, you have a really pretty skull. I think it's your lucky day, believe it or not. You get to say hello to Trevor John's old ankle spanker!"

Victor tried to move, to scream, but whatever black poison those shadows had injected him with kept him rooted. Jesse was approaching the bottom of the hill at this very moment. The blood and venom from the king cobra he had slain was thick on Erra. The sword still blazed with azure light.

Jesse saw Trevor John grinning at Victor as he crept to the bottom of the hill. He saw the dogs frozen in fear. The twin serpent shadows attached to the naked woman's waist were keeping the three pit bulls at bay. Victor remained paralyzed. He was being sexually violated. Trevor John's pants were down. He held his large deformed cock in his right hand, and he was slowly stroking and rubbing it across Victor's stomach. Tears streamed down the old dog walker's face. The woman was masturbating, and the sound of it was like sand paper being rubbed against a black board. Jesse recognized her— another stroller mom from that park bench on Seventh Avenue.

Trevor suddenly howled. His hand flew from his cock to Victor's throat. He punched right through it.

"Holy shit! No!"

The woman's head snapped in Jesse's direction. It looked as if she'd just been woken up. Recognition dawned in her cold, bloody eyes. Trevor John paid no mind. He was worked up, completely lost in lust. The demon took his hand out of Victor's neck. His head came clean off and toppled to the ground. His Indiana Jones hat tumbled away.

Victor's body fell an instant later.

"TJ! He's here!" she screamed in a high and surprisingly girlish voice.

The monster grunted, paying her no mind. His attention was focused on Victor's head as it rolled along the dirt. He was reaching down for it, cock still out. He wanted to debase it.

The woman pointed her finger at Jesse. The shadows began to race toward him. Jesse closed his eyes, and he connected with the pit bulls. Jesse felt a tremendous fear, but also an intense anger. And hunger. He doused the flames of fear, and he stoked the fires of rage into a berserk inferno. The Scorcher opened his new eyes.

"Kill them!"

The pit bulls exploded into action. Menace ran at Trevor John just as he was preparing to place Victor's open mouth on his erect penis. The pit bull bit the back of his leg, and Trevor John dropped the skull. Menace ripped away at the monster's calf. Trevor John bellowed.

Hazard and Killer ran toward the woman. The snake shadows were inches away from Jesse's face, and he lurched back behind a tree.

Hazard knocked her to the ground, and Killer bit down on her throat. She tried to yell as the pit bull chewed her larynx, but only blood came out. The shadows instantly streamed back toward the dead woman. They disappeared inside of her.

Trevor John screamed once again, a horrifying bellow, and utterly inhuman. He kicked Menace off. The pit bull was launched several feet away, off the trail. Trevor John turned and faced the other two pit bulls. He pulled his pants up.

"Attack!" yelled Jesse.

The two dogs stopped chewing on the dead woman and turned to leap at the half-demon. He reached down and caught them by their throats. The monster held the two suspended in midair, his hands a vice grip. They kicked and struggled to breathe.

Jesse could feel Killer and Hazard fading. He closed his eyes and visualized the dogs breaking out of the monster's hold, but that reality wouldn't manifest. Jesse stood, Erra in hand. He would take off this fucker's head right now. The dog walker suddenly felt pressure, then a sharp pain on his left leg, followed by more pressure. He crumpled in agony. A large, yellow python was wrapped around his thigh, fangs buried into his flesh. It was squeezing hard. Jesse swung the blade and cut it in half. Hazard and Killer kicked hard, whimpering in misery. The python slid off Jesse's leg.

Trevor John snapped their necks with a grunt. He threw them off the trail. Menace suddenly bolted from the tree line. He ran low between Trevor John's legs, and he bit up.

Trevor John howled in pain as the dog mauled his ankle spanker. He tumbled and fell over. Menace refused to let go, his locked jaw unbreakable.

Jesse stood, though the pain from the bite and constriction was excruciating. Trevor John managed to somehow twist his body around to face Menace. He grabbed the pit bull's neck. He pressed hard, and it snapped.

Trevor John then picked up his bloody stump. There were tears streaming down his face. He stood on weak legs, holding his penis like a rocket launcher on his shoulder.

The corrupted vessel of Capulus looked at Jesse. It bellowed, then fell to its knees. Trevor John smiled and pointed his severed manhood at Ventura. He spoke in Victor's voice.

"You took off the wrong head. See you in a little while, Messy Jesse. I'll be ok."

He ran away from the Scorcher, cock gripped in his hand like a racing baton.

XVII
JESSE GETS EGGED

The dog walker staggered right, along the hill toward the road. He frantically stuffed Erra into its scabbard, then the scabbard back inside Saul's leather duffel bag. Jesse heard nothing from behind. He scrambled out of the woods and onto the boulevard. The pain from the python bite was intense. Joggers passed him, a Parks Department truck as well. No one paid him any mind.

The dog walker limped as fast as he could past the road and out of the Windsor Terrace section of the park. Jesse tripped over his own feet, and he fell hard. The blade inside the bag rattled as it hit the asphalt. He stood up quickly, leg throbbing. Jesse looked over his shoulder. He wasn't being followed. He scooped up the bag and sat down on a wooden bench. Jesse rolled up his pant leg. Blood trickled from the bite mark. His thigh was swollen.

"Jesus Christ," he muttered.

What am I going to do? he thought. This is too much. He shook his head viciously. An absolute fear was taking over. He looked around the avenue. What Jesse saw with his new vision made him queasy, and it terrified him. He watched a young couple stroll by in matching skeleton costumes, and an old man dodder out of his expensive townhouse. They all radiated a horrible brown light, and it was sickly. It emanated from their auras and stuck to the lush brightness of the world like mud on cotton candy. The black exhaust from passing automobiles oozed along the wind like an aerial oil slick. Deep smog was at the base of this concrete jungle. Jesse hacked and coughed; the smog was funneling inside his lungs like waste from a septic tank.

Jesse stared over his shoulder at the bright shimmering outline of old trees in the park standing tall despite the world's toxicity. The plants and leaves underneath their protection glowed with a warm hue as well, but Jesse could also see shards of mankind's filth ripping at them like malignant nettles.

And somewhere, not too far underneath this ecological and spiritual pollution, were the voices of the dead, clattering in some invisible purgatory. Jesse hoped that he wouldn't see them. He wanted nothing to do with his parents, alive or dead.

The dog walker looked across the street again. The old man was scowling at Jesse, aura now black. Jesse watched a mother and her young daughter walking toward his bench. The mother's aura was shit brown, but her daughter still radiated a whitish light.

"Hurry up! Hurry up! They're waiting for us!" she screamed at the little girl while yanking her hand. The child's aura darkened, the poison of her mother spreading throughout.

"He's blind! His eyes are white!" screamed the little girl dressed like a Dandelion. She pointed at Jesse, and scowled.

"Don't look at him. He's a bum," the mother said irritably, pulling her child forward.

Jesse looked away, and closed his eyes. He could still see an outline of the world behind his lids. Jesse could also feel the enemy coiling around him. They were picking up his scent. Jesse opened his eyes. He watched the serpentine clouds slither overhead. He lowered his pant leg and stood.

The pain was intense. Jesse heard Trevor John's bellow, and it sounded distant. The dog walker swung the bag over his shoulder. *I need to get away from here as soon as possible*, he thought. *I need distance. I'll hop the subway turnstile and go somewhere, anywhere, as long as it's not Park Slope.*

The train station was at the edge of the block, not too far away. Claudia's apartment was across the street, a few buildings up. Jesse hoped she was okay, and he was glad she wasn't around to see him like this. The clouds were pressing down on the Scorcher. They were everywhere, blocking out the warm sun. He felt the blinking eye of Algol mocking him from beyond those sinister swirls of cloud. Its hour was near, and the warmth of Sirius was a January sun submerged in a bed of ice. He would go crazy if he stayed in the Drift any longer. Jesse needed darkness, despite the absolute and immediate danger all around him.

He would walk to the edge of the street, by the train station. It was less than one hundred yards away. Jesse watched the mother and daughter walking up ahead, and they were nearly by Bartel-Pritchard Square. There was nobody else walking in his direction. Jesse looked forward and plotted his course.

He left the Drift, and his body grew heavy once again. Ishum went cold on his arm and transformed into dull tin. His ears popped. The feeling of warmth disappeared, but so did the enemy's aerial encroachment. The pain in his leg increased dramatically.

Jesse slipped into total darkness. He took a deep breath, staggered forward completely blind, and slowly walked several feet. A car horn blared, and he jumped. Jesse suddenly felt somebody brush past him, though the path had been empty only moments before.

"Get the fuck outta the way," mumbled the jogger in a deep voice. Jesse stopped, and the sounds of the runner faded. With total darkness came the overpowering impulse to Drift again.

"No. I have to do this."

Jesse pressed forward, striding as best he could. Jesse knew he was covering space. He had to be halfway there. The dog walker suddenly heard a group of teenagers laughing loudly close by.

"Look at this dickhead. Got a fucking tin arm for Halloween," said one in a squeaky, puberty-laden voice.

"I think he's blind," replied a girl's voice.

"I think you're a slut. And he's a crackhead. Half-man, half-trashcan!" said an older teenager with the husky voice of a fat person. More laughter, then silence. A now ominous silence, as Jesse slowed to a near crawl. There were faint snickers all around him, stifled laughter.

"Trick-or-treat, crackhead!"

The eggs smashed against his chest and legs, stung his hands and face. Yolk dripped down his chin. He almost dropped his bag, and Erra. The laughter was all around him. Jesse staggered forward, and the cackling only got louder. "He's blind you, assholes," the girl said, but she was laughing hard, too.

"Run, run, run!" the kids screamed as Jesse limped forward blindly. They ran as well, the sounds of their laughter soon faded. Jesse kept moving forward. He tripped over a branch, and fell hard once again. Jesse dropped the bag, Erra clanked loudly. He heard people in conversation passing by, but nobody came to help him.

"Gross," said a woman's voice hovering near Jesse.

"What is that shit even doing in Park Slope?" came a male voice in response.

"I think he's blind. Literally, like we're looking at a blind crackhead covered in yolk on Prospect Park West. And he's wearing tin on his arm," said the woman gleefully. Silence, then light laughter. Jesse knew they were taking pictures.

"Hashtag; #blind. #crackhead. #parkslope. #latinoswithtinarms. #beatenandbattered," said the guy flatly. The girl laughed, and their voices soon faded. Jesse tried to stand after several moments, but he couldn't. He slipped back down and lay in the middle of the sidewalk, snake bitten and covered in egg yolk. His bruised face was bleeding, his eyes pale white.

"Let them kill me." Jesse felt empty. No more tears. He started to Drift again. The world became lighter, and overwhelmingly vibrant. His vision was too intense. "This world is shit. There's nothing good here."

Jesse suddenly felt *her*. He couldn't stand the thought of seeing her with his new vision. What if she had a black aura, or even worse, serpent shadows clinging to a debased spirit? What if they had corrupted her, instead of killing her? Jesse couldn't bear knowing. He stopped Drifting, and submerged himself in instant darkness.

"My God, Jesse. Is that you?" Claudia asked, and her voice was trembling. Jesse didn't say anything.

"Are you in a costume?"

She leaned down next to him when he didn't answer. He could smell jasmine on her neck.

"People are trying to murder me."

She hugged him.

"Me too, I think," she said fearfully.

Jesse felt a sharp pang of anger. He tried to stand, and he staggered. She helped support him.

"I'm taking you up to my apartment."

"My bag."

Claudia reached down and picked it up, quickly slinging it over her shoulder. She helped guide Jesse toward her building.

"What's in it?"

"A sword. I dug it out of a cemetery. A Quaker cemetery."

"Is that what you do in your spare time? Grave rob? Is that a hobby of yours?"

"Not a hobby. Just a job. A star told me to dig it up. I'm its champion."

Claudia frowned and said nothing as she led Jesse to her building. Neither yoga teacher or dog walker saw the red Prius barrel onto the avenue and quickly park across the street from Claudia's apartment.

XVIII
CLAUDIA LISTENS

"Where are the brothers?"

Claudia helped Jesse sit down on the couch. "Blake lost them up in Cold Spring. I think he did it on purpose."

There was heavy emotion in her voice. She sat across from Jesse, and stared into his cloudy white eyes. Claudia was dumbfounded.

"I saw him at a bar last night."

"I know. He told me you tried to fight him. He really, really doesn't like you. In a crazy way."

Jesse shook his head.

"He's a piece of shit. I don't care what he thinks," said Claudia.

Jesse sat in silence, blind eyes fixed on Mr. Furley.

"What happened to your eyes?"

More silence. Yolk dripped off the couch. The knight in the corner gazed at Jesse stoically.

"Tell me what happened to you, first. Please. I'll tell you afterward, if there's time."

"Blake accused me of sleeping with you. About an hour into the drive. He just randomly flipped out. I told him we never did anything, and then he started to cry. And I mean bawl. Blake said he really liked me but our love, he was referring to us, 'doomed me. He said 'Love', "I mean…" She stared at Jesse. He said nothing. "The boys were going crazy. They wanted to rip his head off!"

Jesse smiled. He missed the Chow Chows. They were his favorites.

"But he was just blubbering. I mean, I've never seen anything like it. I felt sorry for him."

Jesse didn't say anything. He tried to visualize Claudia's face. It appeared in his mind's eye effortlessly.

"Blake calmed down when we got to his apartment. I still wanted to try and salvage something. He took the boys out for a two-hour walk. Only Blake came back. He told me they ran away. We drove around and couldn't find them, then he brought you up again and he got really weird. We pulled over at the foundry, and he started talking about how *they* were going to torture me, because of you, and he couldn't do a thing to stop it. Wouldn't do a thing to stop it! And then he tried to shake me! I maced him, ran, and kept looking for the brothers. I could hear Blake calling out for me along the trail, threatening me. It sounded like he was with other people, too. I didn't feel safe. I just had to get away. I walked a town over and got on the Metro North."

Rage simmered in Jesse. He tried to control it. Claudia frowned heavily. Tears stung her eyes, and she held them back.

"Then when I got back to Park Slope some creeps started following me, one guy tried to grab my arm and I maced him too and ran a block to the apartment. I was just about to call the cops when I saw you. I just want my dogs back. And I'm running out of fucking mace, Jesse."

Jesse nodded.

"I don't understand. Why me?" she asked.

"The people who want to hurt me know I care about you. So they want to hurt you, too. Blake wasn't lying about one thing. My love *did* doom you."

"Our love," she said quietly. Jesse fought to control his emotions.

"What did you see in him?"

"The future my parents wanted me to have. A life my world told me I should lead. I wasn't really being true to myself, Jesse. I fell in love with you the moment we met. Up by the lake in Prospect Park. Do you remember?"

"Yes."

Silence.

"Do you still have his gift? The statue? Can you bring it to me?"

"Yeah."

Claudia went over to her bureau, and she picked up the statute. She handed it to Jesse. Their fingers locked. Warmth, interrupted only by the unnatural coldness of the demonic woman holding the serpent staff. Claudia took her hand away. He ran his fingers over its grooves, felt its scales and forked tongue. He smashed it against the floor. The pieces cracked and crumbled. Jesse began to Drift. He kept his head down, afraid to look at Claudia. Ishum awoke. She stared in shock at the pulsating gauntlet on his arm.

He told her everything.

Claudia didn't say anything as she sat down next to him on the couch. She watched Ishum pulse. The patina-colored piece of metal flashed bright azure rays as it vibrated on Jesse's arm. Claudia was sure that she could see traces of swirling galaxies in those lights. When Jesse was done after half an hour Claudia looked into his blind eyes and said:

"Why did you lie to me about what happened on the hill? You should have told me there was a snake up there with my dogs."

"I'm sorry. I knew you would call me out on that."

She held his hand gently. *Fuck it*, he thought. Now or never. Jesse looked at Claudia, and saw that she was still beautiful, and she radiated a bright warmth; her outline was tinged with gold. She smiled at him.

"Do you believe me?" he said.

"Yeah."

"Really?"

"You're walking around with an alien slug on your arm. It flashes trippy colors and projects 3D holograms of outer space if you stare at it long enough. I don't think you bought it at Zara's."

Jesse smirked. Claudia kissed him.

"I bet you didn't see that coming," she said, wiping the still-wet blood off his lower lip.

"I can see you now," he told her.

"Well, what's the verdict?"

"Still beautiful. More beautiful."

Jesse sat up straight. His legs felt better. Ishum was beating rapidly. She stared at it, fascinated.

"Is it alive? Is it an alien? Magic?"

"Maybe all three. I'm not sure."

They stared at it. Ishum shined brightly, its rays now cinnabar colored.

"And it's with you forever?"

"Maybe. I hope not."

Jesse stood and looked around. It was still light out, and it felt much warmer. Jesse took Erra out of his duffel bag.

"It's beautiful," said Claudia.

Jesse nodded in agreement. The sword felt great   in   his   hand.

"And this conjunction is supposed to happen tonight?"

Jesse slid the blade back inside its burgundy scabbard. "Yes."

She stared at him, then looked away. Her eyes settled on Ishum once again.

"Where is the ritual going to be?"

He shook his head. Jesse placed the scabbard's golden chain across his shoulders. Erra hugged his back comfortably. He took it off again.

"I'm not sure. I have a feeling it might be at Smith's mansion."

"What are we— "

"We leave New York for the night. Or at least Brooklyn."

Claudia stared at him heavily.

"You want to run and hide? After everything you just told me?"

Jesse swallowed hard. He put Erra on the black chaise. The white light emanating from Claudia was turning a bright red.

"I can't put you in harm's way."

"You already have."

Jesse glared at her. He started pacing.

"You have a car. Let's go to Hudson Valley and look for the— "

She jumped up from her sofa. "Are you serious? You just told me these people want to destroy the fucking world. And you're not even going to try and stop them?"

"Let's just be together."

Claudia stopped Jesse in mid-step. The dog walker's body was extremely warm. His shoulders nearly singed her fingertips.

"We have to do something. They want to destroy this world."

"They may not be able to do it. I think they need me as a sacrifice. They could fail without me."

"They'll still try to murder us, even if they fail tonight. We're just delaying a confrontation."

The dog walker stared at her. He was divided. A part of Jesse did want to confront them— had to confront them.

"We need to call the cops," she said.

"What's to say they don't own the police? Smith is a multi-billionaire."

Claudia frowned, then nodded in agreement. Jesse stood there, feeling those serpentine shadows encroach. The Scorcher heard dead voices, and he felt their misery.

"You want them to destroy it, don't you?" she said "You can't stand what you see. That's it."

Silence. Jesse made no argument. "How bad can it be?"

"It's horrible. Poison. And we're doing it to one another. The dead can't find rest. We're wasting our gifts, collectively."

"It can't be that terrible, Jesse. The gift that Saul wrote about was for everything in our solar system. I mean, maybe it's not about only our species being able to access it. Maybe it's not about our species at all," Claudia said heavily.

He remembered the resilient oak trees and the bright plants underneath their shadows, the little girl with a clean aura, one that was only gradually being contaminated by her mother's state of mind.

"We have to try, Jesse."

The dog walker offered no reply.

"Have you looked at yourself in the mirror with your new sight? Have you seen your own light?"

"No."

Claudia took a pocket mirror out of her purse. She handed it to Jesse. He looked, then closed it quickly. Jesse handed the mirror back to Claudia. She stared at him intently.

"What did you see?"

"What I expected. Nothing." Jesse showed her his blank palms. She stared in amazement.

"That's the price. My reflection's also gone. I have nothing now."

"You have me."

For how much longer, thought Jesse. He held back tears. Claudia hugged him deeply.

"We have to do something, Jesse. And very soon."

She pulled away. Ishum burned bright. Jesse nodded.

"Ok. But for now, I suggest we head somewhere safe. You don't want to leave Brooklyn, fine. I have a place we can go. I think it's secure enough. Both of our apartments are obviously not."

"Ok."

She looked out the window.

"There really are people watching us."

"Yep."

"A mime just waved up at me."

"I bet. We're probably surrounded. But it's still light out, and not everyone is Algol Egregor. I hope. Still, there might be a way. Your car's parked in front? Is it ok?"

"Yeah. Nobody's next to it. And the alarm would have went off if someone tried to mess with it."

"Do you think there's a way we can get to it without being seen?"
Claudia turned away from the window.

"No. We'll just have to be quick. I can shake them if they follow us in the car. Trust me."

"Ok."

"You ready?"

"I'm going to wash up in your bathroom real quick," Jesse said, touching the dried yolk and blood on his face.

"Yeah," and she nodded toward the thin hallway next to the mahogany bureau. Jesse disappeared. Claudia stepped by her window again, peeking out. The mimes were still staring up. Claudia looked away. She stared at the suit of armor in the corner. Claudia touched the knight's visor, and she smiled to herself. Jesse came back into the living room, face clean. They nodded at one another, and Jesse walked toward the chaise. He looked at the duffel bag.

"I have some stuff in this bag that I don't want to take along, Saul's stuff. Can I leave it here, you know, just in case we survive and come back to Netflix and chill?"

She smiled.

"Yeah. Do you still have the keys?" asked Claudia.

"No. Sorry. I think they burned up at the strip club orgy."

"Hey, it happens all the time. Don't beat yourself up over it, babe." Jesse shook his head and grinned.

"My other spare set. Just to be safe," she said, handing them to Jesse. Claudia took the bag out of his hand. She opened the closet and tossed it in.

Jesse strapped Erra across his shoulders. "You want sunglasses?" asked Claudia.

"Sure. Why not?"

She took a pair of large sunglasses out of her purse, and handed them to Jesse. He put them on. Claudia put a black parka over her red flannel shirt, and she walked quickly to the foyer. Jesse followed. Claudia looked through the peephole.

"Coast looks clear."

She opened the door. Jesse stepped out first.

XIX
ESCAPE FROM PARK SLOPE

The hallway was quiet. Jesse suddenly remembered Claudia's creepy neighbor. He looked at 3F.

"Who lives there?" asked the dog walker as Claudia locked her front door. "A doctor named Hank. Why do you ask? " "I think he was spying on me the last time I was here."

" I'm pretty sure he's on vacation. I haven't seen him in over a week." Jesse nodded, looking around the empty floor.

"The stairs. Let's forget the elevator," he said briskly.

They started walking toward the staircase. 3F swung open.

"Ahhhh!!!" Hank hollered. He ran out, swinging a baseball bat at Jesse. The dog walker recognized him at once. It was the bald, freckled man in the crowd that had appeared to watch Ginger's death: Phish T -shirt guy. The cultist who had corrected Smith and been banned from all group activities.

"Motherfuckering dog walker! You ruined my life!"

Claudia stepped in front of Hank and maced him. He dropped the bat. "I loved you, Claudia!" Hank mumbled, clawing at his burning eyes.

Jesse punched Hank in his hands. He could feel the doctor's nose crack underneath the hairy knuckles covering his face. In seconds, Hank was out cold. Jesse glanced at Claudia as he picked up the Louisville slugger.

"You punched him. I didn't know you could punch," she said, surprised. Jesse scowled at her as he rubbed his hand. Claudia looked down at Hank Hawthorne. "Hank was always so sweet. He 'd cover my shifts at the Co-Op when I couldn't make it. Great gynecologist, too."

Jesse gave her a sideways glance.

"From what I hear. He wasn't *my* gynecologist."

"You want the bat?"

"No. Come on. Let's go."

They rushed down the stairs, scabbard bouncing on Jesse's back. He held the baseball bat out in front, and they both looked around at the second floor. It was empty. They walked slowly down the next staircase, then Claudia took the lead. When they got to the bottom steps she halted. Jesse followed suit.

"We walk very quickly to my car when we step out. Where am I going? Which direction am I driving in?"

"South. Sunset Park. Fifty-sixth Street, and between Second and Third," he said quickly.

"Ok. Let's move." Claudia took her car keys out of her purse, she gripped the mace bottle.

Claudia walked quickly across the empty lobby. Jesse followed her out through the heavy front door. The sun was shining brightly. It was balmy outside.

Jesse swung the bat in small arcs as he looked across the street at the trio of mimes. They stood up off the bench, staring at the couple, and then one another. They had serpent-shaped shadows clinging to their torsos, and Jesse could see their auras were as black as soot.

Claudia sped toward her Delta 88. The refurbished 73 Oldsmobile dwarfed the other parked cars on the street. The perfect yellow coat of its paint gleamed like the skin of a solar idol.

There were throngs of trick-or-treaters and partygoers passing by. The mimes approached the curb, but suddenly looked hesitant. There were a lot of witnesses around, and Jesse suddenly became aware of two people wearing Richard Nixon masks in the Prius parked across the street.

The same red Prius that had killed Ginger.

Their shadows were also serpentine, and one of the Nixon's raised his hand to the mimes, halting them. The mimes nodded, and stopped.

The masked figures in the Prius grilled Claudia and Jesse.

"They're gonna tail us," Jesse said. The mimes stood at the curb. The driver started up the Prius.

Claudia opened the driver's door and got inside. She quickly opened up the passenger side door for Jesse, and he flung himself in. Claudia put the Delta 88 in reverse; she slammed hard on the pedal. Jesse stared at the two Richard Nixons as they pulled out of their parking spot.

"The red Prius, huh?" Claudia asked as she drove her Oldsmobile past a slow-moving Dodge Challenger and a yellow Vespa.

"Yeah."

She nodded quickly, and looked in her rear-view mirror.

"Buckle up. Let's shake these Tricky Dicks."

She drove the car along Bartel-Pritchard Square, quickly speeding past that small park in the middle of the boulevard. The Prius tailed them, about fifty feet back. Claudia suddenly pushed the Delta to thirty, and sped quickly down Fifteenth Street and onto Eighth Avenue. There was a Jeep Cherokee and Dodge Durango between them and the Prius.

"I'm going to step on it. Get ready," she said as they waited at the stop sign. Jesse looked at the old Armory/YMCA across the street. It was imposing and strange, a mix of the old neighborhood and new. There were no cars in front of Claudia and Jesse. They had a clear path, for at least two blocks at this point.

"You got it." Both baseball bat and scabbard rested between their seats.Jesse suddenly heard screaming and chaos from behind the Delta. He looked back, and saw two Vespas, one red and the other black, quickly riding along opposite sides of the street. They were violently slamming into pedestrians on each sidewalk. The red Vespa had just run over a man with a mohawk and his girlfriend in a mermaid costume. The couple was sprawled out against the gate of a small two-story home, bloodied and screaming.

"Vespas! Drive, Claudia! Go!"

The light turned green and she slammed down on the gas pedal—sixty. They peeled off, and Jesse nearly flew through the windshield. The seat belt chucked him back. Claudia pushed the '73 Oldsmobile hard along the empty street. Jesse looked back out the window. He watched the black Vespa lose control and crash into the side of a parked SUV.

The Prius turned right on Eighth Avenue and disappeared, but the other Vespa continued to ride hard on the sidewalk. The driver suddenly ripped off her helmet. It was the Asian stroller mom from the park bench. She hurled the helmet over her shoulder and controlled the Vespa with one hand, quickly grabbing something out of her leather jacket.

"She has a gun!"

Jesse heard two pops, and one of the bullets hit the back window. It whizzed past Claudia's head.

"Oh shit! She's aiming at you, Claudia!"

She pressed even harder, and pushed it to seventy. They raced past Seventh Avenue. The Vespa rider accelerated, and with amazing dexterity, managed to keep her gun level. Jesse smirked. The crew of the *Starship Enterprise* was rounding the corner, even drunker than they'd been when Jesse first stepped into Park Slope.

The Vespa slammed into fat Data and a horn-rimmed-glasses-wearing Deana Troi. They were knocked into the street, and the driver accidentally fired her gun up into the air. She fell off the Vespa. The moped flipped, and it hit a beard-wearing lesbian dressed like Riker and her thin Asian girlfriend, who was dressed like Geordi La Forge. Worf, whose cheap makeup made him look more like Rocksteady from *Teenage Mutant Ninja Turtles*, drunkenly screamed and threw up all over himself. Captain Picard was nowhere to be seen.

"Holy shit!" Jesse screamed, head still out the window.

"Did we lose them?"

"Yeah! I think she killed Data!"

"What?"

Claudia pushed the Delta 88 two more blocks in under a minute. Everything went by in a blur. They stopped at a red light on Fourth Avenue. Jesse exhaled heavily. He looked back out the window.

No one was tailing them. No cops, either— so far, thankfully. He stuck his head back inside the Oldsmobile.

"You ok?" Claudia asked. She was breathing heavily, but smirking.

"Where did you learn to drive like that?"

"Back home in Anaheim. Mario Andretti taught me how to drive. He was a friend of my father's. Seriously."

A Ronald McDonald and Grimace were crossing the street. They waved to Claudia. She waved back.

"The Vespas crashed. And we lost the Prius," Jesse said quickly.

There was the sudden sound of a vehicle bearing down. Ronald McDonald screamed in terror as the Prius slammed into him and Grimace. They were both flung across the street. The passenger side Richard Nixon flew through the

214

front windshield and landed hard on the concrete. The Prius blocked the Oldsmobile. The driver leveled a sawed-off shotgun at Claudia's face. She stepped on the gas and rammed the Prius aside with ease. Richard Nixon lost control of the shotgun. He jerked it up at the car roof, and the sawed-off's blast was deafening. The Prius spun as Claudia pushed the Delta 88 forward. There wasn't a hair out of place on her head. Sounds of chaos broke out behind the couple: police sirens, people screaming in the street.

"Sunset Park, right?"

"Yeah," Jesse said, staring at her in amazement.

She drove on. They got to Fifty-sixth and Second in less than ten minutes. The street was empty for the most part. Small, school-aged children dressed up and headed to Fifth Avenue to go   trick-or-treating. "It's that one," he said, pointing to the tenement housing known as the Den.

Claudia drove toward it. Jesse had felt the enemy's grasp diminish as they escaped Park Slope. Still, his sight was a beacon. He would have to lose it for a while. Jesse had a new set of eyes to help him, however. He looked at Claudia and smiled, the sheen of golden light emanating brightly as she drove the car up the block, eight buildings   away   from   the   Den.

215

They stepped out of the Oldsmobile. Jesse quickly strapped Erra across his back.

Claudia locked the doors. "Follow me." They walked hand in hand to the Den.

XX
MARVIN TROUT THE DRUG DEALER
GOES SCARFACE IN THE DEN

They trudged in front of the Den's large gray door, and it swung open before Jesse could take out his keys. The couple stepped back.

"Hi, Jesse." It was Amy, Marvin's elf from Bushwick. Her mousey brown hair was shoulder length and disheveled. She wore no makeup on her small, suspicious face, but wore giant plastic elf ears, and she was half-dressed in her green elven tunic. Her black bra strap showed, and so did her panties. They were covered with images of Link from the *Legend of Zelda* video game series. Her aura was the color of mud. She gave Claudia a dirty look, then grinned at Jesse's yolk-covered sweatshirt and jeans. She grimaced at his bruised face.

"Hey, Amy."

"Did you get egged? And...battered??"

"What gave it away?"

"Damn, Jesse," Amy said, shaking her head.

"Punk-ass kids. Dressed like the cast of *Degrassi High,*" said Jesse, lying."Fuckers! Sorry to hear that. Ready for the party?"

"I was born ready, Amy. Is Marvin here?" Jesse asked nervously, knowing that he would have to explain the stolen gun and costume to the drug dealing LARPer.

"He's on his way. Nobody's here, yet."

She walked inside the Den. The two followed.

"This is my friend, Claudia. This is Amy," he said after the LARPer locked the front door.

They nodded at one another.

"You'd make a good high elf."

"High elf? I don't play swords and dragons. I do love medieval history, though," said Claudia quietly.

"Your friend doesn't know what a high elf is?"

Jesse looked at Claudia, embarrassed. He smiled apologetically.

"Amy and my roommate Marvin run role-playing game sessions here. We and three other people chip in on this apartment. It's kind of like an art space. We call it the Den."

Claudia smiled at him. Jesse looked away.

"An art space?"

"Yep."

"It is nice. Would make a great yoga studio."

Amy looked at Jesse incredulously. The dog walker saw her aura turn red, then black.

"Yoga?" she asked.

"Yeah. Yoga. I teach it."

"So, you *are* into role playing games. Jesse should start taking karate lessons so he doesn't get beat up anymore. Invite the instructor here, maybe. You guys can turn this place into a yoga studio dojo. Toss in some Hopi rain dance classes and you got instant bank."

Claudia looked at Jesse. She rolled her eyes.

"Can I get you guys anything? Some sake? A peace pipe? Kimono?"

"A drink. Just make sure it's not PBR," said Claudia flatly.

"Only Rolling Rock, dear. Jesse?"

"Yeah. Sure, Amy.'

"Make yourselves comfortable."

"I'm always comfortable here, Amy. I pay rent, remember?"

"Yeah, but Marvin says you never chip in on beer. You lose points for that."

Amy walked into the kitchen. She wore a plastic sword across her back. Jesse adjusted his own scabbard. The hilt of Erra was hot in his palm. Ishum vibrated rhythmically along his arm.

"Your little troll buddy has an attitude. I guess all those high school beatdowns didn't teach her a thing," Claudia said, watching her go.

They sat down on a plaid couch. Jesse kept Erra on his lap. The place was decorated for a T.S.R themed Halloween party. Tons of Dungeons and Dragons memorabilia and posters littered the large living room. Skeletal wyverns and dead dwarven dummies hung from the ceiling. Several of the large couches were pushed up against the wall, leaving a huge dance space in the middle of the apartment. Three out of four bedrooms in the apartment were open, only Jesse's remained closed. Claudia looked around and smiled.

"This is the hideout? The safe haven...the art space?"

"This is the Den."

She looked at a poster of a red dragon on the wall. It had giant human breasts.

"You wanted to stay in Brooklyn. This is the best I can offer."

"Where's your room?"

Jesse nodded over his shoulder.

"We'll go inside in a little while. I just need to sit here and rest for a few minutes."

"Are you ok?"

"More or less. I haven't felt them all that much since we left Park Slope. It's still just a lot to take in. That's all."

Amy came back into the living room. She handed out the cans of Rolling Rock. Then she scrutinized the couple.

"Why are you wearing those sunglasses, Jesse? You look like an asshole. Those are lady Ray-Bans."

"I got yolk in my eyes."

"So wash them out. Is that a real scabbard? And a real sword?"

"Yeah. Found it all in a Connecticut Muffin bathroom," Jesse said flatly. He took Erra out of its scabbard. He waved it in front of Amy.

"Awesome. It's beautiful. I have to start hanging out in Connecticut Muffin bathrooms. Only thing you'll find in a bar bathroom is herpes."

Amy winked at Claudia. Claudia scowled.

Jesse put Erra back in its scabbard. He rested it on his lap.

"It's something all right," Jesse said, cracking open the beer and swigging it.

"Am I a little too real for you Miss Thang?" Amy asked Claudia, sipping from her can of Rolling Rock.

"You try too hard."

"You don't try hard enough, Miss Santa Monica."

"Real? You're a thirty-year-old woman dressed up like a leprechaun. I don't know what reality you're talking about. I just wish it was the one where you put on some pants and stopped flapping around that camel toe. That little elf guy on the front of your panties looks like he needs a face lift," Claudia said sharply. Jesse smirked and shook his head.

221

"Jesse! Your girlfriend said I was thirty! I'm going to smoke a joint up on the roof! Tell your yoga friend not to steal anything. I know their kind always do," Amy said, chugging her beer and taking a joint out from behind her plastic elf ear.

"Don't you worry. Her alignment is lawful good."

The elf stormed out of the Den. She slammed the front door.

"My kind? What is she talking about? She's whi—"

"Amy was born in Honolulu. She thinks that changes something, I guess. Don't sweat it." Jesse slowly forced himself to lose the light. The bite mark on his leg started to pulsate with pain. He drank his beer.

Claudia got off the couch. She walked quickly to the window and looked out.

"The Prius is nowhere in sight. No Vespas, either."

Claudia opened her beer and took a long swig. She placed it down on the window sill. Night was beginning to fall. The stars appearing in the sky cast a strange sheen on the asphalt, one Claudia had never seen before. She rubbed her eyes.

"Should we tell your weird friends what's going on?"

Jesse thought it over quietly. He shook his head.

"No. What's the point? They won't believe us."

Claudia looked around the apartment. Her eyes settled on the poster of the red dragon with double D's. She shook her head.

"They won't believe us? Would tossing a unicorn into the story make it more plausible, Jessie?"

"Most of them are atheists. Amy's LARPing is just an outlet for her, an escape. It'll fall on deaf ears. Plastic, or not. Trust me."

"Sure. If you say so," Claudia drank from her can of beer. She looked up at the sky again. "The stars look strange."

Jesse nodded.

"It's close. The meteor. The conjunction."

Claudia frowned and stepped away from the window. She walked over to Jesse's bedroom door. Claudia stared back at him, then looked away. Silence. He felt the Drift calling him as soon as he was out of it, filling him with the urge to fight once again.

They way Erra had felt in his hand— so right. Jesse Drifted again, his sight returned. He couldn't help himself. The presence of Algol Egregor still wasn't detectable. He turned and saw Claudia standing by his bedroom door, sipping from her can of Rolling Rock.

"Can't wait to check out my bedroom, huh?"

223

"I just want to get away from that big-breasted dragon. It looks like a Kardashian. They creep me out."

Jesse stood. He slung Erra over his shoulder, and quickly took out his keys. He left his can of beer on the floor. Jesse walked to his door and opened it. They stepped inside.

Claudia sat on the bed, and Jesse went over to his locker. He opened it, and quickly took out a fresh set of clothes. She took off her jacket and chugged the rest of her beer.

"*The* sombrero," Claudia said, pointing at it. She frowned.

"Yes. Let me get it."

She tossed Jesse the hat. He placed it in his locker.

"We have to focus on protecting ourselves for now, Claudia. But trust me, we're going to expose and destroy these monsters one way or another. They killed a lot of innocent people."

Claudia simply nodded at Jesse and said nothing.

"Sorry. I have to change out of these clothes. I'll be quick," said Jesse, taking off his sweat shirt. Erra was placed gently on the bedroom floor.

"Don't apologize."

He stood concealed behind the open door of his locker, and he quickly changed into a fresh set of clothes. He now wore a clean white Henley, crisp black jeans and fresh socks. Jesse closed the locker. He put his sneakers back on. "I think it's safe for you to stay here. Safe enough. I'm going after them," Jesse said, tying his shoelaces.

Claudia shook her head. He stood up, grabbing the scabbard and placing its golden chain around his shoulders.

"You're not going anywhere without me. So, don't even attempt this routine."

Jesse walked over to the window and looked out. Alien starlight cascaded down from the sky, blanketing the street with deep knots of embedded stellar DNA. He could see the zodiacal properties of sentient star systems falling down like shards of wet crystal, being absorbed by the earth. Jesse could also see Sirius closer than it should ever be, and he saw the Demon Star even closer than that.

"You're really going to make this difficult," he said, not looking at her.

"Yep. So cut the shit."

Jesse sighed. He put his hand on Ishum, feeling its strange pulse. He turned away from the window.

"Why wouldn't you want to speak to your parents if you could? Why are you afraid?" Claudia asked abruptly. She had been thinking about Jesse's encounter with Trevor John in the cemetery. Jesse's face had gone pale, and his voice weak, when telling the story back at her place. And it wasn't so much because of that monster. Hearing his dead father's voice had really rattled him. Jesse looked at her. Golden light shone brightly around Claudia's body. He sat down on the edge of the bed next to her.

"They weren't very good people. They were drug addicts, and abusive. I'm happy they're dead."

Claudia stared at him silence. She took his hand into her own.

"The worse thing my parents ever did to me was get a divorce. And in hindsight, that was probably a good move. What happened?"

Jesse said nothing. He rolled up his sleeve, and showed her a burn mark on his right forearm.

"My dad. He punished me over the stove when I tried to stop him from hitting my mom." He showed her a cigarette burn on his right bicep. "My mom, for not stopping him. Later that night. Plenty more scars. You get the picture, though."

"That's horrible."

"Those scars happened when I was nine. There were a few good years before that. They weren't that fucked up. Then really bad years after that, like   tying-me-up-with-the-dog-in-the-backyard bad. Then killing the dog because he defended me. I stabbed my father in the stomach with a knife after he killed him. He didn't die."

"They were monsters."

"I really loved that dog. He taught me how to be human. I wished upon a star with him. Seriously. Guess that star was listening. Be careful what you ask for. I wanted to have a special destiny."

Claudia put her head on his shoulder. She squeezed his hand gently.

"What was your dog's name?"

"Smokey. He was a husky."

"Can you hear him?"

"Yeah. I've even seen him a few times since the change."

"That's worth something, isn't it? Being able to see the one dead family member you love."

Jesse kissed her. Claudia held his kiss, and she led him down to the mattress. It was six o'clock.

It was ten o'clock when they got up from the mattress.

They were covered in sweat and breathing hard. The bedroom was pitch black. It had been better than ecstasy, beyond physical. She had Drifted with Jesse, and everything beside their own passion for one another had been shut out. The couple sat up, disoriented.

Claudia kept wiping her eyes, but the strange colors wouldn't go away. Jesse had felt a sharp decline in the vibrancy of his vision. It was turned down several notches, close to normal. There was a lot of noise coming from the living room: music and laughter.

"That was amazing," she said breathlessly, "but my eyes..."

Jesse stood, and he quickly got dressed. He listened to the sounds of the party, and he could hear heavy footfall on the roof. His chest tightened. Jesse checked his watch.

"It's ten o'clock. It's been hours, Claudia."

"Is my vision going to stay this way?"

Jesse turned to look at her. Claudia's eyes remained the same shade of deep blue.

"I doubt it. Your eyes are fine. Same color. It may just be temporary. I feel like my sight's been diminished."

Claudia stood and got dressed.

"This is one strange STD, Jesse. And trust me, I've had them all."

Jesse stared at her and frowned.

Claudia smiled. "I'm kidding. Seriously, though. This is all too much; it's like a peyote trip."

"It's been four hours. Do you remember anything besides *us*?"

"No," she said nervously.

He picked up Erra and strapped it over his shoulder. Jesse looked out the window.

"Holy shit."

"What?"

Claudia rushed over to the window.

"We have to get out of here," he said.

There were dozens of cars parked in front of the building. One was the same exact Prius that had tailed them. Wrecked, bullet hole through the top of the roof. It was parked where Claudia's car had been hours before. Her Oldsmobile was gone.

"Park Slope's come to Bay Ridge," he said.

"Well I'll be damned. That was fast."

There was a knock on the door.

"Hey, sex machine! Some guys I ain't never seen before are askin' for you. You want me to tell them you're here?" Marvin's voice.

Jesse and Claudia looked at one another. Jesse put his sunglasses on, and he walked toward the door. The dog walker swung it open. He grabbed Marvin by the neck, and he yanked him inside. Jesse quickly locked the bedroom door.

"What the hell, man!" Marvin pushed Jesse away. He was still dressed up like Raistlin Majere.

"How many?"

"How many what?" Marvin asked.

"How many people are asking for me?"

Marvin looked at Jesse, puzzled. He stared at Claudia and smiled.

"Howdy, ma'am."

"Hey," Claudia said quietly.

"Funny, I thought you would have a louder talking voice what with, um, your vocalizing—"

"How many, Marvin?"

"You serious. I don't know. Like, it's some borin' asshole dressed in a gray business suit."

Smith, thought Jesse. *They've definitely found us.*

"And he's with like two other guys, can't see their faces. They're wearin' snake masks. I don't know 'em. But there's a lot of people here I don't know. And most of 'em ain't even fucking gamers. Just here for the free booze. I don't know who invited 'em. We only got five people playing upstairs."

Jesse stared at Claudia.

"Can you see what color his aura is?"

She shook her head. "Neither can I. Us sharing the vision weakened it in— "

Marvin grabbed the dog walker's shoulder, forcing Jesse to face him.

"What are you talkin' about? First you and Miss Thang nearly blow the roof off the Den for hours on end. I mean, me and Amy are loud but not that damned loud! So loud we had to blast the music before the damn party even started. Now you askin' what color my aura is? Throwin' weird New Age mind fuck shit at me! Listen man, I know you went into my closet and took one of my masks, and my .22! I was gonna wait until the morning to talk about what else you seen—"

"Those people looking for me are not friends, and they're not good people."

Marvin suddenly looked nervous.

"Are they fuckin' cops or somethin'?"

"Some might be. Listen Marvin, they want to hurt me and Claudia. I need you to help get us out of here. How long have they been here? And where are they exactly?"

Marvin studied his face.

"They've been here for like, maybe five minutes. They're in the hallway. Are you carrying an *actual* sword?"

"Yes, Marvin. Can you lead them away and tell them we're on the roof?"

"We're going to try to leave through the front of the building?" asked Claudia.

"There's an exit in the back alley. We just have to get to the first floor."

Marvin stared at the couple. "So you're serious about all this"

"I'm serious, Marvin." Jesse lowered his sunglasses.

"I guess those ain't contacts, huh?"

"I'll explain everything to you if I live through the night."

Marvin the Arch Mage shook his head in disbelief.

"Ok, man. I'm gonna try and get em' upstairs. If I can, then 'Stairway to Heaven' comes on the

231

stereo and you two haul ass out of dodge. You want this? Or you good with the .22?" Marvin suddenly shifted his cloak. He had two Magnum revolvers strapped along his waist band.

"I'm good."

Jesse gripped Erra's hilt. Claudia was already behind him, hand outstretched. Marvin smiled. He handed her the .357.

"Fucks like a demon and ain't afraid to pop off a few rounds. This one sounds like a keeper, Jesse. I got two of my guys packin' heat, you know, just in case some people had the balls to come up here and rob my stash. They already watchin' Grandpa and his crew. Ranger and Paladin, ok? And they look like you, Spanish-lookin' guys, ok? You'll spot em'."

Marvin turned and left the room, and he shut the door quickly. Jesse briefly saw a man dressed up like Alf, break dancing on the hardwood floor. Jesse looked at Claudia. She was inspecting the gun. Her eyes met his own. She smiled.

"Yep." She quickly snapped the revolver's chamber open. It was loaded. She flicked it closed.

Jesse nodded.

"Well there you go. You're up on that too, I guess," he said, smiling.

Jesse touched the door, and he listened intently. The sounds of the party droned on. "Super Freak" by Rick James played. The couple waited silently.

Sudden heavy stomping on the roof. Claudia turned to glance out the window. Amy's body fell past it.

"That elf girl just fell off the roof!"

Rick James asked the Temptations to sing. The gunshots and screams began. Jesse's bedroom door was violently kicked open. It flew off its hinges. Jesse barely dodged it.

Trevor John stepped forward. He was in a Tarzan costume.

"Who's your friend, Jesse? Ain't you gonna introduce us? Uncle Trevor still got his old Ankle Spanker, as you can see. You can't keep a good dick down!"

Rick James continued to sing.

Jesse's reaction was automatic. He took Erra out of its scabbard and sliced at Trevor John's chest. He easily dodged the blade. The half-demon laughed, heading straight toward Claudia, eyes ablaze.

"Get down!" screamed Marvin.

Claudia and Jesse both hit the floor. Marvin shot the hand cannon at the monster, and the bullet hit Trevor John's phlegm-repaired shoulder, spinning him. Claudia pushed his legs forward and Trevor John dropped like a ton of bricks, screaming like an insane Tarzan as he fell out the window. The music stopped. Jesse and Claudia ran from the bedroom, and into pure chaos. There

233

were more gunshots on the roof and two dead partygoers on the floor.

Alf lay in a pool of his own blood, killed while doing the worm.

Most of the partygoers were in hysterics. The plaid couch was knocked over, and people were cowering behind it. One chair was smashed, but the other pieces of furniture were in the same place. There was a bullet hole through the poster of the big-breasted dragon.

"Let us out!" screamed a man dressed like Bazooka Joe.

Marvin barred the doorway.

"I think it's the fuckin' Feds! They started shootin'! They killed my Amy!" The light was playing a whole new set of tricks on Jesse and Claudia's eyes. They had trouble processing what they saw, and when Jesse finally did, he realized that he was absolutely blind to all shadows and auras. There were still at least a dozen costumed people in the room, some in heavy black robes, with blank white masks covering their faces.

Not all appeared frightened.

One robed figure wearing a blank mask was seated calmly on a leather couch, with two very large black bags at his feet. Jesse realized that all of the bedroom doors were open, and the room with the fire escape was just a few feet away from them.

Jesse suddenly heard a familiar bark in the distance, and it didn't belong to the spectral husky. Jesse felt a friend getting closer.

Claudia was having trouble dealing with the sensory overload. Her head was swiveling around a bit, she held on tightly to his shoulder. Jesse took Claudia by the hand, and led her toward the dark bedroom with the fire escape.

"This is fucking Waco! These assholes ain't getting me! They wanna play rough? Ok!"

Marvin was staring around wild-eyed; he looked through Jesse and Claudia, forgetting all about them. Whatever delusional paranoia he had about getting busted by the DEA was now paramount in his mind.

"No one leaves! No one comes in! I ain't goin' back to jail! Shit, I bet it's   impossible to get a good campaign goin' in federal lockdown! I ain't playin' craps the rest of my life with a bunch of degenerates! Watch the door, Hector!"

A tall, Latino elven ranger nodded. He pointed his shotgun at the front door.

"Fuckers killed Amy!"

Marvin Trout ran into his closet. He quickly dragged out the gun crate. He grabbed an Uzi.

"Who wants?"

Nobody moved.

"I just wanna go home!" screamed a man dressed like Pikachu.

"Pussies!" Marvin ran back to the front door.

"Please let us in. We wish to avoid further bloodshed. The police are not coming to help you. Have you heard any sirens?" Smith's voice, calm and boring.

"You are the fucking pigs!"

"Let's go," Jesse said to Claudia.

The robed figure on the leather couch was staring at them.

Jesse led Claudia into the bedroom. He was about to close the door, but it was jarred open with two heavy leather bags, then quickly shut. The couple stumbled forward against the foot of the bed. The figure in the black robe quickly placed the large duffel bags on the floor. Jesse and Claudia turned to face him. He took off his mask, and his hood. There stood a black turtleneck, with a man inside of it.

Blake smiled at them.

"You were making a mistake with this guy, Claudia. I told you. You shouldn't be fucking the help, Claudia." Blake was bug-eyed, yanking at his turtle neck wildly as he spoke. "We could have been a power couple, Claudia! You could have been Facebook friends with Beyonce! But instead, you wanted to fuck around with this quasi-Latino dog walker...deplorable. He's a fucking peasant!"

The couple stared at the maniac in silent shock. "And what can I say to you, Messy Jesse? Um, nice try? You guys are from different worlds, you know? Just wouldn't work. You would have to sign a goddamned prenup, Jesse! But I did keep one promise, Claudia. I brought your little guys back! Yay! Fuckin' puppies! Yay! Well, not all three, the horny one got away. Here they go!" he said like a ring announcer.

Blake quickly reached down. He unzipped the two large bags at his feet. "Nah! I'm gonna give you five seconds to get the fuck out of here, pig!" Marvin screamed from the Den's living room.

Blake took Iago and King Kong out of the bag—dead and stuffed. He patted their heads, grinning.

Claudia screamed. Blake stood and smoothed out his turtleneck. "Babe, they got some great taxidermists up in Hudson Val—"

The bullet blew Blake's head out of his turtleneck. Blood and brains exploded across the room, splattering everything in sight. His body dropped.

"What the fuck!" screamed Marvin.

There was a sudden eruption of gunshots in the living room. Smith and his crew busted through the front door. Marvin's Uzi started blasting.

"Let's go!" screamed Jesse as they ran past the bed to the window.

"Scorcher!" bellowed Trevor John from the living room.

They looked down, and saw only Amy dead on the asphalt. There were people up the block standing in the shadows. One man with a Spanish accent was shouting. "911 put me on hold again! What the fuck is going on over here!"

The couple noticed a small figure run beneath the window.

"Little Dirty Bastard!" screamed Claudia.

He was staring up at them. Little Dirty Bastard howled. "You go first Claudia."

The door was kicked open. Claudia swung away from the window, and she started shooting. Bullets sprayed the empty doorway. Claudia ran out of ammo. King Kong and Iago stared up at them, frozen faces twisted in pain.

"Don't harm the sacrifices! Or defile them!" Smith yelled from beyond the doorway.

Jesse heard Trevor John suck his teeth loudly.

They were streaming in within seconds. *If they take Erra this is all over*, Jesse suddenly thought. He turned and tossed Erra down to Little Dirty Bastard. The Chow Chow barked, and jumped away from it.

Take it and run. Hide. Then find me! Go now! Sirius watch over him! Jesse commanded.

The Chow Chow tilted his head quizzically, then he barked and grabbed the scabbard's golden chain with his teeth. He ran toward Second Avenue, dragging it along.

Claudia cursed and threw the heavy gun at Trevor John.

I'm fucked, Jesse thought, realizing that the Chow Chow probably wouldn't get more than half a block dragging Erra. He suddenly saw a figure dart out of the building.

It was Marvin. He had somehow made it out.

"Marvin!"

His roommate looked up, then away. He paid Jesse no mind. Little Dirty Bastard was at the edge of the corner. Marvin ran past him without so much as a glance. The Chow Chow ran in the opposite direction, with the scabbard's chain in his mouth. Erra clinked behind noisily.

The last thought Jesse had before he was knocked unconscious by Trevor John was that there really were no police sirens. No help was coming. The dog walker fell into deep darkness.

XXI
FAMILY REUNION

Jesse awoke in a lesser darkness, illuminated by torchlight. He was stretched out on a large stone table, unbound. He rubbed his bleary eyes, then touched the large knot on the back of his head, grimacing in pain. It took the dog walker several moments to process his surroundings. The air was dank; it felt like he was underground. Ishum began to throb like a pulse and grow visible as Jesse slowly gained cognizance. The alien artifact had camouflaged itself while he was unconscious.

There was a torch about fifty- feet away, on the wall next to a thin wooden staircase. The surreal way the shadows danced around the torch made Jesse realize that his vision had completely returned. He pushed up on his elbows, and looked around some more.

Jesse was sure he was in a wine cellar, even though he saw no wine bottles. *The* wine cellar—Smith's. The stone slab he sat on was the only thing in the room even remotely resembling furniture, as far as he could tell. It didn't look like anybody was physically guarding him, though

Jesse felt like he was being watched. And not by cameras. He shivered. The dog walker could hear chanting, and not that far off. The cellar itself was quiet. He attempted to stand again, but he couldn't. Jesse licked his dry lips, and he tried to gather his senses. His heart sank. Claudia might already be dead. The chanting was steady and getting louder.

He remembered the massacre at the Den: Claudia, Little Dirty Bastard and Erra.

Jesse didn't need a watch to know what time it was. The conjunction was close, maybe only minutes away. The dog walker could feel it in his bones. He had to act fast. He concentrated on Little Dirty Bastard, and felt his presence almost immediately. Jesse could sense that the dog was anxious from waiting, but not in any immediate danger. He was very close, and outside the building.

Little Dirty Bastard had made it, and so had Erra. Jesse could feel that, too. Sirius had answered his prayer.

The dog walker suddenly heard whispers in the darkness. Spectral faces appeared, gaunt and malicious. The unquiet dead hovered around Jesse, and they cursed his name.

Jesse looked at the cellar floor, and he saw hundreds of snakes slithering on it. A horde of shifting shadows. He did have guards.

"Fuck."

A leering, demonic face drifted out of the darkness, floating just inches away from Jesse. It was his father. The dead junkie's arched eyebrows and large black eyes had been accentuated in death. His slicked back hair dripped blood.

What have you gotten yourself into, Jesse?

Jesse looked away from the shadow.

"Fuck you." His heart thudded against his chest. Jesse hugged his knees.

Thought we'd never see each other again? We have some catching up to do, son.

Jesse was reverting back to his childhood self. The dog walker held back tears; he started to rock back and forth on the giant stone table.

Look at me when I'm talking to you! Look at me, you little pussy!

Jesse felt a cold hand touch his back. He screamed.

Alrighty then Jesse, alrighty then. Your filthy whore of a mother is standing next to me. Say hi to her, at the very least.

Jesse tried to not look, but...

His mother was standing there, and her haggard, twisted face was beaten in. It was unbelievably bruised. She mumbled something.

She said go fuck yourself, Jesse.

His father laughed. The other phantoms wailed.

Get it together, thought Jesse. If Claudia is still alive she needs me. I have to get out of here. Jesse straightened up.

They already raped and killed your little girlfriend. She came harder than when you fucked her. I know. I was there watching you guys.

Jesse looked over the slab, and he saw a clear floor space. He lowered his foot and immediately yanked it back up. The shadow of a rattlesnake lunged at him.

They're coming for you soon. No need to rush death. Let's play catch up and kill some time. Speaking of catch, you remember that dumb fucking dog your mom got you? The one I killed with a baseball bat?

Jesse was staring at the torchlight.

Smokey, right? You named the fucker Smokey.

The smoke. He was concentrating on the flame, remembering how the fire in the bar had seemed to obey his desire when he wanted to scorch the enemy.

Scorch them. I have a flame that burns more than just flesh, he thought.

He's with us, too. You want to see him?

"He's with me," Jesse said flatly.

Silence. He continued to stare at the flame. He felt the spirit of Sirius, and Jesse drew its energy through the fire. The torch light started to kick wildly. Jesse could see hundreds of serpent shadows on the floor, and he could see the suddenly fearful faces of the dead. They whispered nervously.

Stop that. Or I'm going to make you stop.

The flames kicked up higher. Jesse held his scarred forearm out toward the demonic face of his dead father.

"A little fire never hurt anybody, huh? Hell, maybe it's time you tasted some. This is a different flame, though. Special."

Stop!

The flames from the torch spilled onto the ground. They raced with unnatural speed all around the cellar, an instant inferno. Fire covered the walls, the ceiling, and the serpent-covered floor.

The dead shrieked.

Jesse sat on the stone slab, untouched by the fire. He gazed into the flames, controlling them absolutely.

He willed them to stream back into the torch, and they did, all at once. The place smoked, yet his lungs were impervious. It was quiet. Jesse stepped onto the ground. No snake bit at him. They were gone; if they had ever actually been there in the first place. Jesse walked to the staircase and he grabbed the torch. He crept up the wooden stairs. The feverish chanting was louder than ever. Jesse could feel Little Dirty Bastard calling him.

The Scorcher tested the door. It opened.

XXII
NO MORE GATORADE

Jesse could hear Algol Egregor's chanting deeper inside of Smith's complex, perhaps even in the backyard beneath the stars. He walked toward the secret museum.

The Scorcher heard a voice.

Claribel Pendergrass. Her Jamaican accent was now thick, and she sounded angry.

Jesse peeked around the corner. The maid was naked, and she was eating from a bowl of cereal. Claribel was standing alone, and talking to herself between loud chomps. She was complaining about Trevor John, and Gatorade.

"Bumble-clot Trevor John, complain' about Gatorade! 'Get more Gatorade! Everybody tired from screwin.' No more Gatorade, yah, bumble-clot! We just got coconut water!"

Jesse stepped forward. Claribel jumped back, quickly dropping her bowl of Chex Mix. It shattered on the diamond encrusted tiles.

"Help!"

The Scorcher commanded flame. The fire exploded from the torch, and onto Claribel's face. Her screams died instantly. The flames engulfed the woman's skull, the incineration was absolute. Claribel's smoking, headless body dropped to the floor. Jesse looked around. All of the items in the secret museum were gone. Only the display cases remained. Jesse heard barking toward the front of the mansion. He rushed forward, holding the torch like a shield. He stepped up into the foyer, saw that the pornographic pictures remained. His family. Jesse now recognized the Nebuchadnezzar-bearded hipster and the dwarf he had set on fire at the Diamondback.

Jesse ran to the front door, opened it, and shoved the torch out, ready to greet any members of Algol Egregor. The porch was empty. He suddenly heard tiny feet scrambling toward him, and metallic clanging, as well. Jesse reached down to pet Little Dirty Bastard. The Chow Chow dropped the scabbard and licked the Scorcher's hand, tail wagging furiously.

"Good boy. Now go into the park across the street and wait. I'm going to get your master," he said, quickly unsheathing Erra.

The flames from the torch jumped onto the extraterrestrial blade, and they danced along its cyan-colored metal. They disappeared inside the weapon after several moments. The Scorcher strapped the scabbard along his back. Little Dirty Bastard tried to follow him.

"Go!" he commanded, and the Chow Chow scrambled away, then sat stubbornly in front of Smith's mansion. Jesse shut the front door and stepped back inside, Erra in his right hand, torch in his left. Ishum had hardened into pure steel, and it covered his entire left arm.

The Scorcher stopped walking by the edge of the foyer. He willed the torchlight to shrink to an ember, and it did. There were voices up ahead.

"Fuck! Did you leave the door open?"

"No! The fucking maid was up here, man! I mean, what does it matter? There are evil dead people guarding him. Shit! All this screwin' got me dizzy. Why didn't that bitch stock up on more Gatorade!" The accent was Californian. It was Smith's nephew.

"Your uncle's going to kill us!"

Frenzied shouting from the two. The other members of Algol Egregor were still chanting loudly in the rooms beyond. Jesse peeked around the   corner. He saw two robed figures pacing frantically. Smith's bearded nephew suddenly discovered Claribel's headless corpse.

"Ahh, shit! Fuck! He killed the maid! This is fucking bad, man. Do you think he escaped? Fuck!" Smith's nephew was frantic.

"Where is he? All of the initial sacrifices have been slaughtered!" Trevor John's voice, and then his massive form appearing out of the corridor. He wore a scarlet robe, and he towered over his two minions. He was carrying a chainsaw, covered in blood.

Now. Flame. Spread, thought Jesse, stepping into the museum chamber. He held the torch forward. It sparkled and exploded in a spout of blue flame. The minions tried to run. Trevor John started up the chainsaw. He tossed it at the Scorcher, and missed by only inches.The flame streamed over the cultists. They scurried like roaches on fire, then dropped to the diamond-encrusted floor, popping and crackling.

Trevor John took out his cock and pissed a line of defense against the Scorcher's flames.

"You're not strong enough!"

Jesse grinned, concentrated. His torch fire blazed, lanced through Trevor John's vile defense to its point of origin. It raced *through* his urethra.

"It burns!" screamed the monster.

"Yeah. Consider it your last UTI. Say goodbye to your ankle spanker. Freak."

Trevor John bellowed inhumanely and collapsed in the Dog Star's blaze; body motionless. The chanting in the rooms beyond increased to a fevered pitch.

"Come, Capulus! Now! Caput Algol! She comes! Bring the sacrifice!" Smith's voice boomed.

The Scorcher looked down at Trevor John, Capulus. He was burned to a crisp, and he still snapped, crackled and popped. Capulus wasn't going anywhere. Jesse ran forward, following the sound of Smith's droning voice.

XXIII
JOHN SMITH'S CONVENTIONAL ROOMS

Jesse raced past the cellar and into the thin corridor. It had black walls, and not much else. It was a long strip of nothing illuminated by harsh florescent lighting. The Scorcher ran for at least twenty yards. The feverish chanting had slowly been replaced with moans and screams of excitement.

There was a sudden curve in the corridor, and his ears popped. Something had *shifted.* Jesse was hit with a feeling of disorientation, of unreality. The bizarre thought that he had run through the neck of a black hole pounded against his skull. The Scorcher steadied himself, then continued. He sprinted out of the corridor and nearly screamed. Jesse's head slammed into a dead body dangling from the ceiling.

The same harsh light was in this room, and he saw that it was really nothing more than a meat locker. Frost drifted out of Jesse's mouth. He stared up at the flayed corpses. There were dozens of people hanging from hooks along the ceiling.

Only their skin remained, hung like the discarded coils of a serpent. They were all covered in the same tattoos, that spidery alphabet the museum pieces had been inscribed with. These people were sacrifices.

The room was huge. If Claribel had been telling the truth, and there were fifteen rooms in this mansion, then Smith had knocked down the walls of at least ten for this twisted slaughterhouse. Paintings of the runes were all over the blood-splattered walls, along with hand-drawn illustrations of snake people and the Demon Star.

He saw three doorways up ahead, widely spaced across the room by at least twenty meters. Jesse ran past the gray foot of a man that looked like Bono from U2, and he headed toward the middle room. There was a large star sigil drawn in blood the door, and Jessie could hear the loud moans of the cult clearly through it. He also heard Claudia scream in terror. The Scorcher dashed forward.

The doorway was wide, and even though it was dark, Jesse could see that he'd been instantly flanked by two versions of himself as soon as he stepped   through.

There were long strips of mirror on both sides of the corridor. The Scorcher shined the torchlight at his two reflections, which weren't identical at all.

They were trick mirrors, funhouse mirrors. His left side looked heavier, in face and body. His right side was gaunt.

Jesse shook his head, and the reflections did as well. The Scorcher thought he saw the thin curl of a smile briefly edge around both of their lips. Claudia screamed again. Jesse bolted forward, Erra and torch in hands.

The mirror images kept pace for only a short while. His skinny reflection suddenly zoomed out in front of Jesse by several feet. The Scorcher tried to ignore it, but then it stopped running completely. It turned to face Jesse, grinning widely.

It tried to move its arm out of the mirror. Jesse stifled a scream.

He dodged it, and almost fell. Jesse saw that his obese reflection didn't stumble, it kept pace. The Scorcher was getting disoriented, and the hallway kept on going. The parallel mirrors were transforming into something else. He saw glimpses of a black nightmare world in his peripheral vision— stalks of light purple vegetation that looked like splintered finger bones, skeletal and covered in a substance that resembled sawdust and thick mucus. Dark red petals as sharp and heavy as helicopter blades careened out of the purple plant's top, and it lurched out of a ground that looked more like open flesh than soil. There were giant skulking monsters in that twilight realm, testing the strength of those mirrors. Car-sized creatures as much scarab beetle as hyena. Other faceless beasts towered and collapsed over the Scorcher's doppelgangers like a magma-covered slinky. This dark world was drenched in toxic perspiration. The rivers of smoke that sped across the veldt wore jagged crowns as thick as titanium; their humanoid faces carried expressions of hunger and wrath.

The Scorcher saw the purple sky. Its stars belonged in a mausoleum.

He saw himself lift Erra. The Scorcher watched the blade fall across his reflection's blubbery face.

It came off.

He tried to force his eyes away from the mirror. Ishum sparkled wildly, and the psychedelic lights it projected seemed to sizzle against the mirror world and push away the darkness, momentarily.

The mirrored corridor was squeezing thin; it looked like he wouldn't be able to move forward. There didn't appear to be an exit, just a small point ending in the conjoined mirrors of this nightmare room.

He had the very real fear of stepping into it, and never being able to get back out. The Scorcher looked quickly at both walls of mirrors.

One of the car-sized hyena insects had his skinny doppelganger in its mouth, and it was ripping him apart. The heavier reflection on the Scorcher's left side was still running next to him, face hacked off. It no longer held its Erra. "Fuck," the Scorcher whispered, as he slowed his jog to a creep.

The space forward was only a few feet wide. The mirrors were extremely close to his shoulders, and he could feel the mutilated reflection of himself on the left side trying to break out of its world. Jesse bolted forward, and fell to his knees.

The parallel mirrors were constricting him. He could nearly smell the rancid realms hidden behind them.

He heard Claudia's scream again, close, and up ahead. The Scorcher saw a black hole between the conjoined mirrors, several inches away. Ishum was shooting psychedelic pyrotechnics as if it were the Fourth of July; the rays were slamming against the twin mirrors. The darkness pushed away from them like a vampire fleeing dawn.

He lowered the flame and crawled forward, right next to the mutilated face of his double. Jesse screamed, and the reflection laughed. Its hand shot out of the mirror, grabbing the Scorcher's left shoulder with its blackened, freezing fingertips. The creature tried to yank him in.

Ishum exploded in an indigo blaze, and the double screeched, losing its grip. Jesse stabbed up under its left arm with Erra, and the blade stuck the phantom through its elbow. Flame and small bursts of light exploded from the sword. The grotesque specter howled in pain and fell back into its hellish world.

Jesse crawled out of the mirror's hollow corridor.

XXIV
A SHADE OF THE GORGON

The Scorcher stood several feet away from the open door of the courtyard. The chanting of the acolytes was at its loudest here. There was a locked wooden door on his left-hand side, and a wide-open entryway on his right. The hole he had crawled out of was less than four feet across. He shook his head in disbelief.

The Scorcher kindled his torch, and he readied Erra. Ishum went still, its cold, hard steel encasing the entirety of his left arm. He stepped through.

The large courtyard was flanked on both sides by the empty backyards of unoccupied townhouses. Jesse wondered if Smith owned all of the real estate on the block.

The Scorcher looked ahead and nearly screamed.

He saw Claudia. She was strapped to a giant marble chair shaped like a serpent, naked, and covered in a dark green paint. There were blue sigils painted on her skin, as well. The serpent crown was on her head, and the diamonds from

257

that monstrous tiara sparkled brightly in the torch lit courtyard.

The original vessel lay dead at Smith's feet, blood flowing from her throat. The dark-haired Middle Eastern woman had been viciously stabbed to death. There was a stone altar, and two other serpent-shaped marble chairs behind it, on opposite sides of Claudia. All three were inscribed with the glyphs of the fixed stars they represented: Mirfak, Algol and Capulus.

Smith stood in front of the altar in a black robe. An enormous, brightly colored serpent shadow radiated around him. It spun in circles like the ouroboros, devouring its own tail. The corrupted vessel of Mirfak was wielding a tremendous amount of energy.

He held a giant cobra high above his head. The nude cultists, what looked to be almost a hundred of them, were fornicating on the grass of the giant yard. Smith, orchestrating the ceremonial orgy, moved the snake back and forth, and the bodies of Algol Egregor moved as it moved.

Smith suddenly looked at Jesse, and his face twisted in shock. He then slowly smiled.

"Step forward, dog walker. Claudia lives, and *she* has been chosen as the vessel for our goddess. We thank you for bringing her to us. She will be freed from this earthly coil. We will all taste the immortality of Ra's al-Ghul, soon enough. Not you, however, and not the other that has been rejected," Smith said as he spat on the corpse.

"Jesse!" screamed Claudia.

The fornicators on the grass paid the Scorcher no mind.

"Let her go."

Jesse held the torch forward. He swung Erra in small circles. The blade sang.

"I'll assume you've disposed of Capulus. Good. He was ultimately irrelevant. It's too late now. She's almost here, and my power has grown immeasurably!"

The multi-colored shadow of the ouroboros was swinging around wildly. The corrupted vessel of Mirfak was manic, he was losing control, perhaps for the first time.

"I can feel myself inside of them all!" Smith moved the coiled cobra from over his head. It straightened as his arm did. The twenty-foot-long serpent was as unbent as a staff.

Smith pointed it at a random follower.

"Stand! Cast yourself into flame!"

A thin, naked man with a short red beard stood up. He ran over to a torch, and he shoved his face into its flame. Smith laughed, and the man screamed. He continued to burn himself, however.

"I'm the Scorcher now! I can do your job better than you!" Smith giggled as the man dropped lifelessly away from the torch, face blackened and burnt to a crisp.

Claudia was trying to pull herself out of the chair. Jesse ran forward, kicking aside moaning flesh on the cold grass. Smith pointed the cobra at Jesse. The Scorcher froze in midstride. He couldn't move.

"I was always bigger than Bilderberg, dog walker. They were fools! They never understood true power! I've slapped Henry Kissinger, spat upon George Soros! Those little men and their little ideas, their feeble aspirations. Less taxes! More taxes! Robotics! War! Space exploration! Fools! Petty fools! They never understood me. They never understood the power that flowed through me and my clan. The so-called rulers of this planet fighting over a world that wants to die."

"I can feel her getting closer, Jesse!" Claudia screamed.

The Scorcher tried to move again, but he was paralyzed. The acolytes continued their act of ritual sex on the cold, filthy ground.

"Fuck their religions! Those worshipers of transient gods and devils. Idiots who knew nothing about the laws that inspired their deities. Disgusting. Adulating the feverish projections of a few desert outcasts with sunstroke! We go further! I am the corrupted star of Mirfak, and I will show you their Christian devil and savior."

Ishum and Erra were sparkling brightly, fighting against Mirfak's stellar will. Jesse still struggled to move. Smith laughed. The Scorcher watched in terror as Smith's Lucifer appeared and stood next to its conjurer— red-skinned and horned, sharp tail whipping wildly around its black goat legs. A scarlet-eyed Prince of Hell, wet pupils poetic and dreamy, shining brightly on the face of a snout less fox. He smiled and bowed. Lucifer picked up the dead Middle Eastern woman, and he danced with her. He stuck his forked tongue out at Jesse, and then he abruptly let the corpse drop.

Smith laughed insanely. He continued to point the cobra at the Scorcher. "Should we give the little imp a pitchfork? Better yet, a buddy?"

The devil suddenly stuck his red hands inside his own mouth. He began to rip his face back.

Claudia screamed again, her eyes began to close. They jerked back open in fear. She was staring up at the sky, not the Devil.

Lucifer ripped his face back, and the bearded visage of Jesus Christ looked out: blue-eyed, with blonde shoulder-length hair, he looked more like a Bee Gee than a Middle Eastern prophet. His eyes were the same as Smith's Lucifer, however, despite their difference in color. They had the same gleam of poetic insanity, wet and turgid.

"We are going with the Hallmark card version of Christ, dog walker. The standard issue, as they say. If you want to see him in a different color I suggest you file a complaint with Human Resources. Then perhaps I'll show you a Negro Jesus! Smith giggled. Jesus stared out at Jesse, and he smiled placidly. His body was still covered in Lucifer's red skin.

"If I had more time I'd show you Buddha, Mohammed, and L. Ron Hubbard. But she draws near!"

Smith took the cobra away from the Scorcher. He nearly fell and dropped Erra. He breathed in heavily. The corrupted avatar of Mirfak pointed the serpent at the centuries old vision of Western religion, and it exploded in a cloud of dust. The stench was like a rotten hamburger doused in petroleum.

"Rise! Rise, and begin her song! The hour is now!"

Algol Egregor instantly arose in perfect unison. They began to chant in an ancient, watery language.

The Scorcher pushed himself forward.

"Jesse! Something's happening to me!" screamed Claudia.

A chill passed through the crowd, and the chanting stopped. Jesse's torch went out, and the starlit sky suddenly blackened. They were in an absolute darkness. Jesse could see nothing, even with his special sight.

"Jesse, help! I can feel—"

"No!" the Scorcher screamed.

Claudia's voice trailed off. The sky's darkness faded, and Jesse saw Smith bowing at the feet of Claudia, the cobra above his head. She was now transformed. The same face, but her eyes were a startling green, and her hair was jet black with scales on the tips. They rose and slithered along invisible currents.

She stared down at Smith, then up at the sky. Her glowing green eyes considered the empty altar, then the absent seat of Capulus. The Cosmic Over-Soul frowned through the face of Claudia. It was horrific.

Jesse began to sob. He stumbled back toward the building. Nobody stopped him. Jesse stood at the edge of the door.

"Mother!" screamed the acolytes.

"The goddess has come," whispered Smith.

She stared down at the corrupted vessel of Mirfak, and something was communicated between them.

Smith shrieked. "But my goddess, I am enough! The Scourge of Sirius is present! He will be sacrificed!" Smith was blabbering, and he accidentally dropped the serpent on the ground. He looked at the goddess in terror, and screamed, then covered his face defensively.

The radiant ouroboros circling Smith began to shrink. Claudia turned to face the empty stone table again. She looked back down at the disciple who had failed her. Smith's hubris had doomed him.

She pulled Smith up by his gray hair and he screamed. The serpent shadow around him completely disappeared.

The shade of Algol hacked at Smith's neck with Claudia's bare hand, and it came clean off his shoulders.

"Holy shit!" shouted a naked reveler.

The gorgon threw Smith's head against the empty altar. It exploded and the stone table cracked in half. She then gazed at her followers.

Jesse ran back inside the mansion. The Scorcher heard screaming, then a strange crunching noise. He peeked back out. The bodies of Algol Egregor had been completely petrified. Rows and rows of the naked cultists were twisted and stooped in obscene and terrifying poses.

"Step out, Jesse. Let me see you," said the gorgon in Claudia's voice.

"I'm sorry, Claudia."

Jesse stuck the torch back into the yard. He closed his eyes and spread its flames. The courtyard was burning within seconds.

Jesse raced back inside the mansion. The flames followed him, and so did the shade of

Algol. The inferno had begun.

XXV
THE SCORCHER

Jesse looked at the two doorways next to the mirror room hollow. He went over to the open entrance on the left-hand side and glanced in. Pitch black, yet Jesse could sense shifting figures. Large, serpent shadows that would coil around you and never let go. Not even in death.

He ran to the closed wooden door and tried to open it. It wouldn't budge. This had to be the normal passageway; he doubted the other two were premier routes. He raised Erra and easily cut through the door. The Scorcher heard a loud hiss by the courtyard's flame-licked doorway. He turned to see Claudia's unburnt hand emerging from the inferno.

Jesse bolted forward into the most normal looking room in the mansion. A huge den, furnished like an expensive hotel suite. The photographs that lined its walls, however, were cheap pornography, much like the pictures of Smith's family in the foyer. He saw an open door up ahead. There was frost streaming out of it. It was the meat locker.

"Help me, Jesse! It said she'll let me go if you sacrifice yourself. The fire won't stop her!" cried Claudia's voice inside his head.

The Scorcher heard another voice up ahead in the meat locker. It was Saul's. He followed it.

"You have to kill Claudia, Jesse. You'll free her soul. The Demon Star will take her to a place worse than Hell if you don't. It'll take you and anyone else it kills within the next few hours, during the conjunction, and for all eternity. Decapitate Claudia!"

The Scorcher ran past a pair of dangling twins: two identical brunette women who may have once been beautiful. Their skins began to quiver.

"How do I know it's you, Saul?"

Jesse stumbled forward, and he almost fell into a decapitated corpse that was hanging upside down. It was the only body that hadn't been flayed.

"Cause you're looking at me!" Saul screamed. His shadowy figure stepped out from behind his headless corpse.

"You have to destroy her. Run! Get ready in the next room. I can slow her up, Jess. The veil is still thin. Run!"

Several flayed skins began to quiver and drop to the floor. The Scorcher watched in horror as the twin suits of flesh slithered toward him.

"Damn it, run Jess! She's doing that!"

The Scorcher ran past the soul of his dead mentor. The pieces of flayed skin slithered after Jesse. The flames glided into the meat locker, and so did the gorgon. "Run faster, Jesse!"

"Be reborn in my dead heat. Submit," an inhuman voice echoed.

The voice almost stopped Jesse dead in his tracks. The twin suits of skin jumped towards him. Ishum pulled Jesse's body around to face the monsters, and Erra danced in his hand. He sliced them both, and Ishum froze them in midair. The sliced chunks of skin were violently propelled past Saul, and right into the gorgon's path. She petrified them and they fell harmlessly to the floor.

"Go!" Saul called again.

He willed the quivering bodies of the sacrificed from their hooks, hurling them at the Demon Star's avatar. One nearly hit her, yet she managed to slide away quickly on her scaly legs, which were unnaturally bent backwards.

Jesse ran through the corridor. The gorgon glared at the corpses. Her giant pupils burned an emerald green. Then came the deafening sound of petrification and broken stone as the quivering hunks of cadavers began to fall from the ceiling. As he raced through the corridor, the Scorcher also heard Saul's ghostly wail.

Ishum shined on Jesse's arm brighter than it ever had. Erra was on fire. Jesse hit the middle curve of the passageway. His ears didn't ring this time, nor did he experience any disorientation. He didn't have time to wonder why. There was a loud explosion inside the meat locker, then a monstrously loud rattle along the corridor. The Scorcher's feet felt as if they were burning, then like they were not there at all. He looked down and saw that he was gliding forward. Shifting indigo wings flanked the sides of his New Balance sneakers, hurtling him away from the gorgon. He suddenly stopped outside of the corridor and past the cellar. The feeling in his feet returned, and his sneakers were normal once again. The Scorcher leaned against the wall by the doorway, panting in exhaustion. He readied Erra, then heard a whistle, and a chainsaw revving up. Trevor John, burned to a black crisp, bolted toward Jesse from the museum chamber.

"You can't kill me!" he bellowed. Jesse heard a ghostly howl. He watched Smokey manifest behind the monster.

He leaped on top of the half-demon, and savagely bit the back of its neck. The dead husky's eyes shined bright. Trevor John's chainsaw swung wildly. Jesse suddenly heard the hiss of the gorgon several inches away. Ishum pulled his arm up. The galactic Over-Soul glided forward.

The badge of Sirius dazzled with the fierceness of a supernova, then it became a black mirror. It reflected the gorgon's own vile soul back at it. The monster froze for a moment.

"I'm sorry, Claudia," and the Scorcher spun around from the wall. He lowered Ishum, and swung Erra at the gorgon's neck. Its head came off.

Smokey continued to bite the back of Trevor John's charred skull. Jesse reached down and instinctively grabbed Claudia's head by her scale-tipped hair. The dead husky jumped off Trevor John's back. The monster stumbled forward. The Scorcher pointed the gorgon's head at Trevor John.

The hulking creature turned to stone right before Jesse's eyes. Trevor John fell, but he didn't crumble. The husky howled, and drifted away with the plumes of smoke that were quickly filling up the front of the mansion. There was a loud pop, then the sound of fabric being ripped apart all around Jesse. Claudia's head shook violently, then it went still.

The Scorcher looked down at her blonde hair, then gazed into her deep blue eyes. He closed them, and sobbing, placed her down into the flames. Ishum dimmed as Jesse walked past the petrified body of Trevor John.

He looked down, and to his horror saw Trevor John trying to break out of the stone.

"Motherfucker!" he screamed, swinging Erra down on the half-demon's neck. He severed the head. Trevor John exploded in a blaze of crimson light. Jesse saw the horned insect shadow of the Thing screaming, and withering in the flame.

The Scorcher staggered forward, more blinded by his tears than the smoke all around him.

XXVI
A PARTING

He watched the mansion burn down with the Chow Chow at his side, across the street in Prospect Park. The Scorcher had walked right past the arriving fire trucks and cop cars in a swirl of smoke. Only Little Dirty Bastard saw him. Ishum's camouflage was complete.

The dog walker cried, and only stopped when he saw the spectral vision of Claudia appear before him. Little Dirty Bastard barked and wagged his tail. They followed Claudia into the woods of Prospect Park.

The couple spoke until the sun rose by the lake, and when she started to fade, when the veil between their worlds started to descend, they made a promise to one another. Claudia kissed Jesse, and he could feel her lips on his own.

XXVII
THE CURSED DIARY
OF A BROOKLYN DOG WALKER

*E*rra's been buried where Saul originally found it, in the wilderness of the Ozarks. He instructed me through dreams to bring it to Missouri. I now mark Ishum, which has left my body and transformed into the book once again. I'll be burying it soon with Erra, as well. I now pass this legacy onto you, whoever you might be, when the Good Star decides to summon you.

Be it fifty years from now, or five hundred.

The conjunction's passed. The Demon Star's been defeated.

It's been two months since that night. I left the next morning. Ishum told me that Algol Egregor remains omnipresent, and they haven't all been vanquished. I'm marked. They'll be coming for me, along with the police. It's a miracle that I've lasted this long. Still, I believe the surviving sects are in disarray.

They've lost this century, I believe. I've taken Saul's small cabin in a secluded section of the Ozarks, away from civilization. It's beautiful here.

MICHAEL REYES

Little Dirty Bastard is with me. I'll soon lose most of the Drift. Still, even in blindness I can see the stars brighter than I ever had with my regular vision. I will see Claudia again one day, possibly very soon. We made a promise to reunite in death. May this world always be under the protection of our second Sol, Sirius.
Jesse Ventura.

Jesse pulled his bloody fingertip away from the page. He tossed Ishum into the ditch on the hill, then quickly buried it next to Erra.

It was dawn. He stared directly at the sun, smiled, closed his eyes. Jesse turned away from the foot of the giant sycamore. He saw Little Dirty Bastard staring at him impatiently.

Jesse picked up his leash, and he was quickly led up the hill by the Chow Chow. The psychedelic colors of the Drift began to evaporate. The darkness encroached.

Jesse got to his cabin and sat down on the porch. He pet Little Dirty Bastard's head gently. He looked forward, into blackness, now blind. Yet, Jesse began to see light trickling down from the heavens.

He looked up at the sky. It was now brilliant, filled with an alien brightness. Jesse shuddered in fear, then closed his eyes.

Michael Reyes is an author from Brooklyn living in the Bronx. He writes a dark urban fantasy series named *Clock's Watch*.

ALSO AVAILABLE FROM
NIGHTMARE PRESS

RETRO HORROR

Twelve tales of old-school drive-in-style horror

WHOOPS! I WOKE THE DEAD
by Joseph Rubas

A teenage girl with an ancient spellbook accidentally wakes the dead on Halloween night.

VAMPIRE SERIES OF EXTREME HORROR BOOK TWO:
THE GRAY MAN OF SMOKE AND SHADOWS
by Todd Sullivan

A rogue vampire seeks revenge on her abusive
uncle while another vampire hunts her.

VAMPIRE SERIES OF EXTREME HORROR BOOK ONE:
BUTCHERS
by Todd Sullivan

Vampires hunting vampires in the no-holds-barred
bloodfest set in Korea.

CHAINSAW SISTERS
by Jacob Floyd

An amnesiac woman believes her dead sister is talking to her through a chainsaw, asking her to seek revenge against the men who killed her.

NIGHT OF THE POSSUMS
by Jacob Floyd

JACOB FLOYD

Man becomes roadkill as mutant opossums rise up
and attack a small Kentucky town.

Thank you for reading! If you like the book, please leave a review on Amazon and Goodreads. Reviews help authors and publishers spread the word.

To keep up with more Nightmare Press news, join the Anubis Press Dynasty on Facebook.